Alan H .
He left s
father's farm, spending his spare time sailing on the
orfolk Broads and writing nature notes for the *Eastern
Evening News*. He also wrote poetry, some of which was
published while he was in the RAF during the Second
orld War. By 1950, he was running his own book
hop in Norwich and in 1955, the first of what would
become a series of forty-six George Gently novels was
ublished. He died in 2005, aged eighty-two.

The Inspector George Gently series

Gently Does It
Gently by the Shore
Gently Down the Stream
Landed Gently
Gently Through the Mill
Gently in the Sun
Gently with the Painters
Gently to the Summit
Gently Go Man

Gently Go Man

Alan Hunter

Constable & Robinson Ltd
55–56 Russell Square
London WC1B 4HP
www.constablerobinson.com

This paperback edition published by Robinson,
an imprint of Constable & Robinson Ltd, 2011

A copy of the British Library Cataloguing in
Publication Data is available from the British Library

ISBN: 978-1-78033-148-5

Typeset by TW Typesetting, Plymouth, Devon

Printed and bound in the UK

1 3 5 7 9 10 8 6 4 2

To
NICHOLAS FLOWER
in acknowledgement of his interest in this book

The characters and events in this book are fictitious;
the locale is sketched from life.

CHAPTER ONE

TEENAGER KILLED AFTER JAZZ SESSION

HIGH-SPEED CRASH

FIANCÉE SERIOUSLY INJURED

The road leading to Latchford is one of the big A roads and it has a stretch of five miles as straight as the crease in a sheet of paper. It crosses a shallow depression so you can see one end of it from the other and at the westerly end there's a dead tree which is called the Gallows Tree. When you see the Gallows Tree you've got it good for forty furlongs. At around the ton it's going to last you three minutes, more or less. You come out of the fir plantations which are the end of Latchford Chase and then you twist her hard up and she blasts off like a shell. And it's real, man, real. You're pushing the ton before you know it. The tree comes opening up like a flower. It sends you, the way that tree gets bigger.

Returning from a weekly jazz session at Castlebridge last night eighteen-year-old John Lister, a plumber's mate from Latchford, crashed his motorcycle at high speed in the notorious Five Mile Drove stretch. Lister was killed outright with multiple injuries. His fiancée, Miss Betty Turner, who was riding pillion, is still unconscious. The wreckage of the machine was found a hundred yards from the body. Latchford Police have appealed for any witness to contact them.

But Latchford itself isn't any big deal. Not to jeebies like us who were mostly born in the Smoke. It was just a one-street pull-up in the middle of nowhere, with a market square off one side and a station and a bridge. That was before they started in to make it an overspill area, before the factories moved in and all this neighbourhood-planning stuff. Now there's more people live here and more going on here, but I'm telling you, it's still a one-street pull-up at the bottom. After the slog you've nothing to do, there isn't no place to go. There's a flea pit the size of a cupboard and a weekly hop and ten pubs. Sure, they're building it all now, it'll be a topspot one of these days. But just now there's nothing to it. You arse around and want to scream. You like to cut up every so often, go for a smash or a pitch in. Or you burn up a bit of road. It's like that. It's the way it gets you.

Latchford Police are appealing for any witness to contact them. The accident occurred at approximately midnight.

Well, we just weren't born to it, that's the way it is, man. They never ought to have moved us up here in the first place. It's bad enough in the New Towns, they haven't got it, they're stupid dull. But they don't give you the creeps like this deal does. What I hear of Siberia it's like that around Latchford. You ride a mile out of town and there's nothing there at all. You dig? Just nothing. Roads, houses, we don't have them. Not even grass we don't grow, it's all stones and bracken and fir trees. There's a road coming and a road going and that's about it, I guess. And for miles it goes on. You're shut up. You're in a prison.

A detective is waiting at Miss Turner's bedside. Latchford Police are appealing for any witness to contact them.

There's a square, one of these club leaders, hands me the patter about Latchford. How it used to be the Brum of the Stone Age, he says. Used to come here from all parts to get their axes and arrow-heads and there's a place called Shuck's Graves which is one of their old mines. And man, it doesn't change any. Maybe that's why it's so creepy, huh? You get out there on your lonesome and not nothing would surprise you. You see a little guy shamble past you, he's wearing a skin and carries an axe, and that fits, he's part of the scene, it's you who don't belong round there. All the time you've got that feeling. All the time you don't belong. It's like you can't wake up or something or you've got yourself lost, you know how it is?

POLICE SEARCH FOR MYSTERY RIDER
SECOND MOTORCYCLE INVOLVED
TEENAGERS QUESTIONED

Latchford Police today revealed that they have reason to believe that a second motorcycle was involved in the fatal accident at Five Mile Drove on Tuesday night. A spokesman says that the tyre-marks at the scene of the accident suggest that the dead youth, John Lister, was forced off the road by an overtaking vehicle. Today they have been questioning some Latchford teenagers who own motorcycles and also attended the jazz session at Castlebridge. Detectives continue to wait at the bedside of Lister's passenger, Miss Betty Turner, who has still not regained consciousness. The police are appealing strongly for any witness to come forward.

Then you dig this one-street graveyard. It used to be an important outfit. A sort of capital or something if the square was giving it straight. Had their kings here and the lot around a thousand years back, then some geezers came and pitched them and burned the whole deal flat. So it's spooky, you get it, first and last it's spooky. And the people here are like the place. We don't get on with the people. They don't want us, we're just muck. They've had us dumped on them, that's it. We might as well be a lot of nigs the way they give us the breeze. And then these squares who go the other way and try to be the big brother – Jesus Christ, we could murder them. We've had a pitch at one or two.

TEENAGER AT POLICE STATION

ASSISTING THE POLICE

Laurence Elton, 17, a Latchford builder's labourer, spent several hours at Latchford Police Station today assisting the police in their inquiries into the fatal accident at Five Mile Drove on Tuesday night. Elton, who owns a motorcycle, attended the jazz session at Castlebridge. The police took possession of a black leather riding suit and a pair of riding boots. The vigil continues at the bedside of Betty Turner.

There's only one thing, man, there's the road out of here. You had to go miles from the Smoke for a road to burn. When you've got the creeps on you you can kick it out to the road, then you can twist her round and go for the real. You know about that? You know the real when you touch it? Some of them smoke sticks or get the touch from a jazz scene. But not me. I'm a cool jeebie. I get the touch on the road. I want that tree growing up for me till it blacks out the sky. And then I could go, man. I could take it and keep going. I could go into the black because the black is the real. But not yet, I want to think about it, I want to go on touching. But one day I'll do it. I'll drive that tree into the sky.

DEAD MOTORCYCLIST: PROGRESS

TEST ON CLOTHING

Latchford Police today reported progress in their investigation into the fatal accident at Five Mile Drove on Tuesday night. Laboratory tests have been conducted on certain clothing in the hands of the Police. Laurence Elton, the teenager who has been assisting inquiries, was driven to the Police Station from his home in Paine Road this afternoon. The condition of the injured girl, Betty Turner, is said to be improving.

* * *

They fetched him into Inspector Setters' office at about nine p.m. that night. He was trembling and screwing up his eyes because the lights in the cells were very dim ones. He was five foot ten and slim built. His crew cut made his hair look paleish. He'd got brown eyes and a snubbed nose and a girlish mouth and a big round chin. He was wearing a black windcheater with white-striped sleeves and tight black jeans with varnished brass studs in them. His shoes were fancy sneakers. He sported a ban-the-bomb badge.

'Sit down, Elton,' Setters said.

Elton sat on the chair in front of the desk. To the right of the desk sat Detective Sergeant Ralphs. The desk had some report sheets and other documents on it.

'Have you done some thinking, Elton?' Setters asked.

'Yuh,' said Elton. 'I've done a lot of that.'

'Are you ready to give us the truth, then?' Setters asked.

'I've given it to you,' Elton said. 'I never busted Johnny off.'

'That's your story and you're sticking to it?'

'It's the truth,' Elton said. 'I didn't bust him.'

'And you didn't see the crash. Though you were passing right at that time.'

'I don't know that,' Elton said. 'It's only what you've been telling me.'

'Now I'm going to tell you something else,' Setters said. 'Then perhaps you'll sing a different tune.'

He peeled off a report sheet and laid it to one side. Elton watched him. His cheeks were flushed, he kept pressing dry lips togazz-sessether. Setters picked up a statement and flicked over a page. He sat a moment or two scanning it. He laid it down on the desk.

'So you were a pal of Johnny's?' he asked.

'I was his pal,' Elton said.

'On Tuesday night?' Setters asked.

'Yuh . . . Tuesday night too.'

'Then listen to this statement,' Setters said. 'It's just come in from Castlebridge.'

He began to read the statement.

'Statement made to Castlebridge Borough Constabulary by Edward Frank Bagley, 23 St John's Road, witnessed by Detective Constable Hill. "On the evening of Tuesday 22nd September I proceeded to the Ten Spot Milk Bar in Prince's Street with Thomas Cook, Mary Stebbings, Harry Robson, Nina Black, and Jill Copling with the purpose of attending the weekly jazz session held there. We arrived at about half-past seven and parked our scooters in the park opposite the milk bar and there met John Lister, Betty Turner, Sydney Bixley, and Anne Wicks, who had ridden over from Latchford. While we were talking to them a young fellow who I later learned was Laurence Elton rode up to park his motorcycle, and when he saw Lister he walked up to him and began to be offensive. Lister tried to ignore him and walked away towards the milk bar, but Elton followed him across the road and I saw him make a threatening gesture. Then Lister went into the milk bar with Betty Turner and some of the others, and Elton came back to finish parking his motorcycle. With regard to the order in which they drove off afterwards, Lister and Betty Turner went off directly after the jazz session. I saw Elton go for his motorcycle about five minutes later."'

Setters stopped reading. He looked at Elton and waited. Elton ungummed his lips.

'Yuh, that was nothing,' he said.

'You were going to hit him,' said Setters.

'No,' Elton said. 'I wouldn't have pitched him.'

'It doesn't sound like it,' Setters said.

'I'm telling you straight,' said Elton.

Setters rapped on a sheaf of papers. 'I've got supporting statements from all those kids. There was only Bixley who didn't see it. He's your only friend, Elton.'

'Yuh, but it was nothing,' said Elton.

'You hated his guts and you know it,' Setters said. 'Shall I tell you why? Because he pinched your girl. Her sister told me, and it's all down here.'

Elton dragged up one of his sneakers. He twisted his hands in his lap.

'It's just the same,' he said. 'I didn't bust him and I didn't see it.'

'Right,' Setters said. 'Now we'll come to the real business. You've had your chance to change your story, and it's the last one you'll get. I'm going to tie you into this job till even Houdini couldn't get you loose. You've heard of Houdini, have you, Elton?'

'Yuh,' Elton said, 'I've heard of him.'

Setters took back the report sheet he'd taken off his pile. He held it out in front of him with both his arms flat on the desk.

'This is a report from the forensic laboratory at Castlebridge,' he said. 'The subject of it is those leathers and riding boots you kindly lent us. You did a nice job on them, Elton. You sponged them and polished them up a treat. But it didn't work, Elton. You ought to have burnt them, you know that?'

Elton didn't say anything.

'Yes,' said Setters, 'you ought to have burnt them. Then you wouldn't have a report like this one to explain away. Because you know what it says, don't you, Elton? It says there was blood on those boots. You'd sponged it and polished it off the surface, but we dig a little deeper than that.'

'There's a cat I ran over—' Elton began.

'Hold it, sonny,' said Setters quickly. 'As from now what you're saying is evidence and may be introduced in court. It breaks my heart to tell you this, but you needn't say a bloody word. But what you do say we're taking down. Have you got that clear, Elton?'

'I got it clear,' Elton said.

'So now you can tell us about the cat.'

'I ran over one,' said Elton. 'That's how I got the blood on my boots.'

Setters nodded very slowly. Sergeant Ralphs had begun to scribble. Elton licked his gummy lips. It didn't seem to wet them much.

'Yes,' Setters said. 'That's a very nice explanation. People do run over cats and splash some blood about, Elton. But do you really want to know something? That wasn't cat's blood, sonny boy. It was blood like yours and mine. It was human blood, Elton.'

'I cut my hand,' Elton said.

'Do you know your blood group?' Setters asked.

'I cut it at work,' Elton said.

'We know your blood group,' Setters said.

'I don't know anything about blood groups,' Elton said. 'I cut my hand on a bit of piping.'

'But we know your blood group,' Setters said. 'And it's not what's down here in this report. What's down here is Lister's blood group. It was Lister's blood you had on your boots.'

Elton gummed his lips up close. He swayed a little in the chair.

'Any comment?' Setters asked.

Elton didn't make any comment.

'And there's another thing,' Setters said. 'We took some casts back there by the body. We took two casts of a size nine boot with a Goodyear sole which had had pedal-wear. A bit of blood there is on those casts. There had to be. The boots had paddled in it. Like somebody had come to have a close look, to make sure that Lister was really a goner. But it wasn't you, was it, sonny boy? You didn't bust him and you didn't see the crash. You just sailed by like a bat out of hell, then you sponged your boots and you went to bed. And you left the girl there to die if she wanted to. That was a sweet touch, leaving the girl.'

Elton made a sort of pushing move with his hand. He was squinting a bit. His mouth was open. He made a funny swallowing noise.

'I'll tell you,' he said.

'Yes,' said Setters. 'You'll tell us.'

While Sergeant Ralphs kept scribbling it down.

* * *

Setters sent out for coffee and a packet of sandwiches. Elton didn't want to eat but he got down a cup of coffee. Setters offered him a cigarette but he didn't want that either. His cheeks kept going from white to red and he was shaking so he spilt some coffee. His eyes were fixed ahead of him below the level of the desk, he didn't look to see when he tilted the coffee-cup. Setters smoked. He couldn't keep from watching Elton. Setters was fifty. This was his first case of murder.

They finished the coffee and Ralphs took Elton's cup from him.

'Go ahead,' Setters said. 'And remember it's evidence.'

Elton cringed as though he were expecting a blow from someone.

'Yuh, I stopped,' he said. 'I saw him. I stopped.'

'What did you see?' asked Setters.

'I saw his bike,' Elton said. 'On the verge it was. All twisted and bashed about. There was bits of it in the road. The lamp, the battery. I saw the lamp first. Then I saw the bike.'

'How fast were you going?' asked Setters.

'About in the nines,' Elton said.

'And you saw the lamp?' asked Setters.

'Yuh, I nearly hit it,' Elton said.

'Go on,' said Setters.

'Then I saw the bike,' Elton said. 'So I hauled up and made a turn. I rode back to look at the bike.'

'Only the bike?' asked Setters.

'That was all I'd seen,' Elton said. 'I didn't see Johnny then. He was back down the road. I got a torch, I had a look. I could see it was his bike. And the engine was hot. I burned my hand on the engine.'

'So?' Setters said.

'I could see the marks,' Elton said. 'The verge was scuffed up for yards, I kept walking and walking. Then I found the spot where he'd busted off. Betty's handbag was lying there. But I'd gone right past him. He was right over in the fence.'

'Then?' Setters said.

Elton hesitated. He was making sweat.

'Then I searched along,' he said.

'What did you do when you found him?' Setters said.

'I – I looked him over,' Elton said.

'How do you mean, you looked him over?'

'I looked him over. He might have been alive. I had to look,' Elton said.

'And he wasn't alive?' Setters asked.

'He was all smashed up,' Elton said. 'Head smashed. Legs. Everything. Blood. I got in it. Didn't see it. You never know what it's like. I couldn't stand it.' He gave a sob.

'So you decided he was dead,' Setters said.

'Yuh, he couldn't have been alive.'

'And you did what?' Setters asked.

'I looked for Betty. I had to look.'

'Go on,' Setters said.

'She wasn't so far. She'd come off sooner. She was near the place he'd busted off. In some bushes, she was.'

'And she was still alive,' Setters said.

'I didn't know,' Elton said. 'If I'd known I'd have done something. She looked the same. Smashed. Blood. I didn't go too close to her.'

'Friend of yours, wasn't she?' Setters asked.

'Yuh. Friend of mine, she was.'

'So you didn't check she was alive?'

'I didn't want to go close,' Elton said.

Setters leaned back in his chair. His eyes were hard on Elton.

'Now,' he said, 'we'll hear what the big hero did about this. He finds a crash by the roadside. He finds two of his pals smashed up. What does big hero do? Just keep telling me, Elton.'

Elton shrank a little more.

'I was scared,' he said.

'Scared of what?' asked Setters. 'They were dead, you tell me?'

It's always scary out there at night,' said Elton. 'All those trees and rough country. All of a sudden I couldn't take it. I couldn't. I'd had enough.'

'Sounds good,' Setters said.

'It's the level. I'm telling you. I was scared. It hit me sudden. Seemed they were still hanging about there.'

'So you drove in and told us.'

'Yuh, I could have done,' Elton said.

'But you didn't. And why didn't you?'

'I saw the truck coming,' Elton said.

'So what?' Setters said.

'I saw it coming,' Elton repeated. 'Back there by the tree, I saw its lights come up and over. So I knew it would get reported. I didn't need to tell you. I ran down back to my bike. I was scared. I went home.'

'You were scared all right,' said Setters.

'I told you I was. I couldn't take it.'

Setters made a face at Ralphs. Ralphs shrugged his shoulders. Setters rubbed the side of his cheek as though he were testing it for a shave.

'And you didn't bust Lister, you say. Nor you didn't see it done.'

'No,' Elton said.

'Though he pinched your girl.'

'That wasn't anything,' Elton said.

'You wanted to pitch him for it, didn't you?'

'It wasn't like this,' Elton said. 'We're always pitching. It don't count. A pitch don't count for much with us.'

'You carry a blade, sonny boy?'

'We don't go for blades,' Elton said.

Setters rubbed his cheek again.

'Would a jury buy it?' he asked Ralphs.

Ralphs gave another shrug. He doodled a little in the margin of his notebook. Setters kept on rubbing his cheek. At last he pressed the button on his desk. A constable entered. Setters pointed to Elton.

'Take his lordship back to the cells,' he said. 'I've got to cogitate on his future.'

When he was gone Setters said to Ralphs: 'He's good, that kid. You could almost believe him.'

'I was believing him mostly,' Ralphs said.

'Yeah, mostly,' said Setters. 'Just mostly, that's all.'

He lifted the phone and began to dial.

'We'll have the Old Man in on this,' he said. 'I had that charge lined up on a hair-trigger, but I've got the seconds. I don't feel like pulling it.'

★ ★ ★

FURTHER POLICE APPEAL FOR WITNESSES

WAS JOHN LISTER MURDERED?

ELTON RETURNS HOME

POLICE SEARCH FOR MISSING WITNESS

LAURENCE ELTON DISAPPEARS

VANISHES AFTER QUESTIONING

YARD CALLED IN LISTER CASE

SUPT. GENTLY TAKES OVER

NO TRACE OF ELTON

There was a kid killed on that road, man, and the screws made a big deal of it. Threw the curve that one of his pals had busted him off the verge. How square can you get, man. They wouldn't never understand it. You can't sit in a screw-shop explaining the touch to the screws. But that jeebie wasn't busted, you can take it from me, man. He was over the ton when he went, he was getting it, that's all. A big-shot screw came down from the Smoke to try to make the curve stick, but he didn't fool nobody, not even himself. Johnny Lister was the kid's name, man, and he died on the road.

CHAPTER TWO

THE BLACK ROVER 75 was coming up the road from Castlebridge and it slowed by the Gallows Tree and pulled over on to the rough near it. The driver sat for a moment smoking his pipe, a big man with big shoulders, dressed in a casual dark suit and wearing a dull coppery tie. He was in his early fifties, his face was rugged, archetypal. The mouth was full and the jaw squared. The nose was shapely and strong. The eyebrows were heavy, a little greyed. His hair was mid-brown, greying too. His eyes were hazel and had a mild expression. He was Superintendent Gently. He was from Homicide.

He got out of the car and walked over to the tree. It had been a very large ash tree but now it was dead and greyly sere. The ground beneath and round it was bare and was scattered with paper and rubbish, and there were many tyre-marks and signs that meals had been eaten there. It was on the crest of a slight ridge and the view was extensive on all sides. The dark brecklands stretched about it, softly undulating to their horizons.

The brecklands were a sandy, stony waste, and they were dark because of the scurfy heath. Their levels were broken by scattered fir trees, sparse, sand-polished, melancholy.

He stroked the bark of the tree, stood looking down the straight road. It was nearly noon of an October day and there was plenty of traffic on the road. Every few moments came the buzz of a car separating itself from the anonymous stream, then dying back into it again to be replaced by another. There were trucks, too, heavy articulateds, groaning by like tall ships. And motor-cycles, several of those: he counted eleven in fifteen minutes. All the long five miles the traffic was scuttling and burrowing and glittering. As far as the black line of Latchford Chase. As far as the cross on Setters' sketch map.

He knocked out his pipe on the tree and glanced back at the road he had travelled. An Austin-Healey was shooting towards him, but after that was a break of half a mile. He got back in the car, started the engine, waited some moments for the road to empty. He eased the clutch, drew away, slid through the gears, gave her the gas. The Healey was well ahead now, too far for him to hope to catch it, but the road behind it was clear and he could let the 75 rip. It went up fast on the downward grade. He was into the eights very quickly. Soon he was flickering into the nines, which the 75 didn't often reach. Her engine was straining a very little, the slipstream boomed in his ears. She was steering lighter than he liked it, but not enough to cause him worry. It was fast, very fast. She was right up in the nines. The

Healey wasn't losing him now, he was sitting tight at his distance.

Then the Healey slowed for an overtake, came leaping back down the road to him, and he felt a surge of disappointment as he was compelled to ease off. Still, he was drifting along in the sevens, he went through hard on the Healey's tail. They were gunning again directly and pushing back to the nines. He felt the excitement spark in him, found himself wanting the extra ten. That line of trees was coming too leisurely, he would like it striding along to engulf him. But he sensed the recklessness in the excitement and he thrust it down under his usual phlegm. It wouldn't do, he was here to register. The excitement was sought as a point of reference.

They came up on a line of traffic and had to kill it, this time for good. The Healey kept bobbing out impatiently but each time it was baulked. Back in the fives and sixes, padding along like town traffic. No more champagne. No more temptation. They reached the trees and passed a lane that came in diagonally from the left. Setters had marked it, and Gently drove now with one eye on the verge. And soon he spotted it: a violent welt that carved acutely through grass and earth, exploding into a ripped crater and continuing in dragging gashes and raw weals.

He stopped, reversed, and bumped on to the verge. He relit his pipe. He went to look.

'What's your first move?' Setters asked, dropping sugar lumps in his cup of coffee.

'I'll see Elton's people,' Gently said. 'Then I'll talk to Lister's mother.'

'Elton's people don't know anything,' Setters said. 'I've got them covered in case he contacts them.'

'I'd like to see them all the same.'

'I'll take you round,' Setters said.

They were in the lounge of the old Sun, which was still the best hotel in Latchford. Gently had invited Setters to lunch after their conference at Police H.Q. The conference had lasted two hours and had been attended by the Chief Constable, and Setters had formed the private opinion that the proceedings had bored Gently. He was surprised to be asked to lunch. He didn't know yet what to think of Gently.

He drank some coffee. 'We thought the girl would've helped us,' he said. 'Might've remembered some point, like the way chummie was dressed. But no, not a thing she remembers. Only him boring in on them. We're lucky at that, I suppose. Makes it open and shut when we get him.'

'You asked her about Elton?' Gently said.

'Yes,' Setters said, 'I asked her. Seemed to worry her, talking about Elton. Said she'd done him wrong or something. But she won't have that Elton did it.'

'And she'd been doping.' Gently said.

Setters nodded. 'The doc soon tumbled to it. Reefers. Those damned kids get them from somewhere.'

'Any other cases of that?'

'Two. It's the London kids who do it.'

Setters was a large-boned parrot-faced man with dark grey eyes and a bald, conical crown. He had long, sad lines down each side of his mouth which had no expression. He was sharp as a fish-hook.

'Have you had much trouble with motorbikes?' Gently asked.

'Yes,' Setters said, 'since the overspills came. Not much before that. The local kids here are tame enough. You get a wild one now and then. But not the way it is now. Not with jeebies and that stuff.'

'What's this jeebie business?' Gently asked.

Setters said nothing for a moment. 'I get to hear,' he said presently. 'I get to hear what goes on. You know about the Beat Generation?'

Gently shrugged. 'What I read.'

'We've got it here,' Setters said. 'We've got the beatsters in Latchford. Only here they call themselves jeebies, don't ask me what for. The teddy-boy stuff is right out. Now it's jeebies and chicks.'

'Yes.' Gently nodded. 'There's a lot of it goes on in town. It was the name that puzzled me.'

'Guess it's local,' said Setters. He lit a cigarette, lifted his head to puff smoke. 'I've run across it a lot,' he said; 'it's what this case is mostly about. And I don't get it all, that's a fact. I don't get above a half of it. It's not gangs any more, though there's gang stuff in it. And it's not them dressing all sloppy, and not washing or cutting their hair. Beards, that sort of caper, that isn't it either. There's something funny got into those kids. They just don't figure like they used to.'

'There's still hooliganism,' Gently said, 'petty crime, and violence.'

'Yes,' Setters said, 'that too.' But he sounded as

though it didn't mean much. 'I've talked to most of them,' he said. 'All the kids who've got bikes. If it wasn't Elton I'm stuck, or there's some damned good lying going on. But I don't think so, that's my hunch. I think they don't know much about it. They don't even believe that Lister was busted off. They think we're cooking it to make it tough for them.' He filled his lungs, drove the smoke out. 'You know the angle they keep giving me? They think that Lister did it on purpose. Just for the kick. What do you make of that?'

'It could be a smokescreen,' Gently said.

'Yes,' Setters said, 'it could be. But it isn't, they really believe it. And they don't know anything. That's my hunch. 'So you're sticking to Elton,' Gently said.

'I'm sticking to him,' Setters said. 'Until I hear something different. Elton is chummie number one.'

They collected the 75 from the park and drove into the new town area. It lay south-east of the old town, which was mainly stretched along a narrow High Street. It looked raw and unsettled. It was like an exhibition job; it might have been run up for a season's stand, not really intended to be lived in. It had all come out of an architect's sketchbook; it was thrown there, not grown there. Maybe it photographed and took prizes, but it hadn't character, only design. It was the design that stood out. It looked like ideas without finality. It had come easy, it could go easy, it didn't mingle or take root. It was using local brick and pantile and making both look anonymous.

Paine Road was a shallow crescent of blocks

containing six houses. They were brick built with a plastered first storey and reeded wood panels along their fronts. They had wide upper windows with ugly functional frames. The ground floor was taken up with a garage and a utility room and a dustbin cupboard. They were separated from the road by a narrow grass strip intersected by paths and driveways of concrete.

They parked by number 17. Setters rang. The door opened. Gently saw a stout, middle-aged woman, with a small, sharp nose and a thrusting chin.

'Oh,' she said. 'It's you again, is it? Well, he ain't home yet.'

'This is Superintendent Gently,' Setters said. 'He'd like to talk to you, Mrs Elton.'

She shrugged a plump shoulder, stood back from the door. Setters led the way up some plastic-treaded stairs. At the top, at a small landing, Mrs Elton nudged open a door. They went into a long room with long windows facing the road.

'Sit down,' Mrs Elton said. 'You've been in and out enough. I'm just making a cup of tea. S'pose you can do with a cup, can't you?'

Setters declined. Gently accepted. Mrs Elton went through into her kitchen. All this while some jazz had been playing somewhere up on the next floor. The room they were in was shabbily furnished with a pre-war suite and some painted furniture and was at this end a lounge and at the other a dining room. One of the carpets, however, was new, and there was a new self-tuning television set. There were pottery ducks flying on the wall. The small one had had its head knocked off. In a small painted bookcase inconveniently placed were some newspaper-Dickenses and a pile of magazines.

Mrs Elton slid open a service hatch and pushed through it a tea-tray. Then she re-entered the room. She poured the tea, splashing it noisily. She handed Gently his cup, took her own, sat down on the settee.

'It's Maureen,' she said, jabbing a thumb towards the ceiling. 'Don't know what *she's* coming to. Worse than the other one, Maureen is.'

'Maureen's Elton's sister,' Setters explained.

'Yes, twins they are,' said Mrs Elton. 'Blitz babies the pair of them. Born to trouble, were them two. Now what do you want to ask me what I haven't told you already? I haven't seen no more of Laurie. Nor I ain't heard from him neither.'

'The superintendent,' said Setters, 'is from Scotland Yard.'

'You don't say,' said Mrs Elton. She looked at Gently with satisfaction. 'Me, I'm from Bethnal,' she said. 'Harmer's Buildings, we lived at. My old man was a porter when we was down in Bethnal, but now he's in the building lark. Doing all right for himself, he is.'

'And you've just two in your family?' Gently asked.

'Just two,' said Mrs Elton. 'And that's enough, I can tell you. Two's enough in these days.'

'Have you relatives in London?' Gently asked.

'Dozens and dozens,' said Mrs Elton. 'There's my two sisters and our old mother and aunts and uncles and nephews and cousins. And I know you've been to look them up cause they've writ and told me so. And Laurie ain't gone to them. Though maybe he's with his pals in Bethnal.'

'What pals?' Gently asked.

'Kids,' said Mrs Elton. 'Chums. He ran around like the rest of them, he knows the backsides of Bethnal. But I don't say you'll find him there. It's just a guess, that's all. There's nowhere much to hide there, and where there is you must have looked. So I keep thinking of Bethnal. Bethnal's where I'd look myself.'

Gently nodded. 'What about his pals round here?' he asked.

'Well,' said Mrs Elton, 'they're like they are, that's all I can say. They're a quieter lot, in some ways. You don't get none of that fighting in gangs. Maybe there's only one gang here, I dunno. But they're quieter.'

'And his girlfriends?' Gently asked.

'Same with them,' said Mrs Elton.

'Was he very friendly with Betty Turner?'

'Was he,' she said. 'He was stuck on that one.'

She hoisted herself off the settee and refilled the cups. The jazz upstairs had stopped, instead one heard a mournful wailing.

'Maureen,' said Mrs Elton. 'Gives me the pip that girl does. You should see her room, a proper pickle. And that lazy. Never works for long.'

She sat again, smoothed her skirt.

'Proper stuck on her,' she added. 'I liked her too, she was a decent girl. It's a shame what's happened, that's what I say.'

'How long were they friends?' Gently asked.

'Oh, quite a time,' said Mrs Elton.

'When did they stop being friends?'

'About last Whitsun,' Mrs Elton said. 'He'd just got his new motorbike, on the never-never, that is. He was going to take her to Yarmouth, then for some reason she wouldn't go.'

'Was he upset?' Gently asked.

'Nearly howled,' said Mrs Elton. 'Went off somewhere on his own and didn't come back till early morning. Did him a world of good no doubt, it doesn't harm them to get the brush-off. I reckon a brush-off is educative. When you're young, that is.'

Gently drank and put down his cup. 'And after that?' he said.

'He soon cheered up,' said Mrs Elton. 'Laurie isn't the boy to brood.'

'Did he mention Lister?' Gently asked.

'Not that I remember,' said Mrs Elton.

'Did he have a new girlfriend?' Gently asked.

'Not particularly he didn't,' said Mrs Elton.

She looked squarely at Gently. She had surprising blue eyes. Her face was puffy and her cheeks pallid. She would never have been good-looking.

'Are you married?' she asked him.

Gently shook his head.

'You should be, a man like you,' she said. 'And my son isn't a murderer.'

Gently stirred. 'We're not saying he is . . .'

'No,' she said, 'you haven't said it.'

Her eyes brimmed over. She felt for a handkerchief. She dabbed at her eyes for a moment. She put it away.

'It's like this,' she said firmly, 'there ain't no harm in

Laurie, really. He's a good boy, he always has been, he's always kind to his old mum.'

She used the handkerchief again.

'And he's never been in trouble, really. Just the games they all get up to. He pinched a bike when he was a nipper. And he's steady he is, he holds a job. There's never been no complaint there. He'd grow out of it. He's a good boy. There's no harm in him. Not none.'

'He's been in fights, I'm told,' Gently said.

She nodded. 'Fights, yes. He's been in them.'

'He was put on a year's probation,' Gently said.

'It's nothing,' she said. 'Not a year's probation.'

'And a traffic offence. A speeding fine.'

She shrugged, looked at him. She twisted her mouth.

'But he ain't wicked,' she said, 'he wouldn't kill no one. Not my son wouldn't. Not Laurie.'

'Would he smoke reefers?' Gently asked.

She looked away. She said nothing.

Upstairs the jazz was going again and feet were slouching on the floor. A trumpet moaned, the saxes blared, drums thumped out a naïve rhythm. They all glanced upwards.

'I think I'd like to talk to Maureen,' Gently said.

'You're welcome, I'm sure,' said Mrs Elton.

Her lips tightened. She rose.

Maureen came in. She was a hefty girl with a tangled mop of honey-coloured hair. She wore a black shapeless sweater which came below her hips and had a sagging turtle-neck, calf-length jeans, and ballerina sandals. She was not made up. She had dirty nails. Her hands looked grubby and the fingers were nicotine-stained. Her expression was sulky and she didn't look at the visitors. She sat down languidly on a pouffe, spreading her legs.

'So you are Maureen,' Gently said.

Maureen didn't contradict him. She looked boredly out of the window, shaking her hair back from her eyes.

'I'd like you to tell me about Laurie,' Gently said. 'About his friends and the things he did. And about Johnny Lister. And Betty Turner, about her.'

Maureen gave her hair a flick.

'You answer him, my girl,' said Mrs Elton.

'Like why should I?' said Maureen.

'Because I tell you to,' said Mrs Elton.

'And give Laurie away?' said Maureen.

'Never you mind about that,' said Mrs Elton. 'Just you tell him what he wants to know. And none of that stupid talking, neither.'

'These squares,' Maureen said.

'You hear what I tell you?' said Mrs Elton.

Maureen drew up a leg, scratched her ankle a few times.

'Like he was a jeebie,' she said. 'Cool. He went for it way out.'

'Tell me about jeebies,' Gently said.

'You wouldn't dig it,' said Maureen. 'If you're a square you're a square. It's nowhere jazz to a square. But Laurie was cool, he went after it. Shooting the ton, that sort of action. But like I say you wouldn't dig it. So what's the use me talking?'

'Where do they meet?' Gently asked. 'Do they have a club house or something?'

'Man, you're the most,' said Maureen. 'You ain't

getting it at all. Like it isn't a club or that jazz, it's the way people are. Like squares and jeebies. You're either one or the other.'

'And Lister was a jeebie?' Gently asked.

'Him too,' Maureen said.

'And Betty Turner?' Gently asked.

'She's a chick, man. A cool chick.'

'How did *she* go after it?' Gently asked.

'Like she shot the ton,' Maureen said.

'Like she was smoking sticks?' Gently asked.

'Like she may have done,' Maureen said.

'And what about Laurie,' Gently asked. 'Wasn't he smoking sticks too?'

'He went for kicks,' Maureen said. 'He went way out for wild kicks.'

'Would you pass me your handbag?' Gently said.

'Like help yourself,' said Maureen, grinning.

He took the drawstring bag she had brought with her and made a quick check of the contents. He handed it back. She grinned again. She took out a cigarette and lit it.

'Man, I've known brighter squares,' she said.

'Take that smirk off your face,' said Mrs Elton.

'Like my face is my own,' Maureen said. 'I don't have to keep it straight for nobody.'

Gently watched her for a moment. She puffed smoke towards him. She flicked her hair once or twice. She kept her eyes away from his. He said:

'How well did you know Lister?'

'I saw him around,' Maureen said. 'I wasn't never a chick of his. I saw him around, like that.'

'Didn't he used to be friends with Laurie?'

'Till the Turner chick,' Maureen said.

'Who else was he friends with?' Gently asked.

'Lots,' Maureen said. 'We all liked Johnny.'

'Name some of the others.'

'Sure,' Maureen said. 'There was Sidney Bixley and Dicky Deeming. And Jack Salmon. And Frankie Knights. Like he used to be way out with Dicky, but Dicky's the coolest. We dig him big.'

'Tell me about Dicky,' Gently said.

'Like I have done,' said Maureen. 'He's crazy, he's wild, he's way out with the birds. We meet at his pad sometimes. He's got a pad in Eastgate Street. We've got a combo and make with the music – man, it's the wildest. I go for Dicky.'

'He's some sort of a writer,' said Setters. 'A long-hair. I checked him.'

'He's nice,' said Mrs Elton. 'He ain't one of these silly kids.'

'What does he write?' Gently asked.

'Booksy jazz,' Maureen said. 'He fakes some action for the papers, but that's nowhere stuff, it isn't it. Like he writes some wild poetry, jazz that really makes the touch. And he's writing a book too. Man, that book is the craziest.'

'And he was a special friend of Lister's?' Gently asked.

'He's friends with all of us,' Maureen said. 'I've got big eyes for that jeebie. But he don't never have a regular chick.'

'You've seen him since the accident?' Gently asked.

'Sure,' Maureen said. 'I saw him last night.'

'What does he think about what's happened?'

'A kick,' Maureen said. 'The mostest.'

'A kick for Lister?'

'Like what else?' she said. 'Like he was touching and heard the birds. When you shoot the ton you get to touching. It sends you, man. Like you must go.'

'How old are you?' Gently asked.

'I'm seventeen,' she said. 'Like Laurie.'

'And where did you pick up all this jargon?'

'Not from me, she didn't,' said Mrs Elton.

Maureen flipped her hair again, gave her other ankle a scratch.

'Squares,' she said. 'Always squares. It's a nowhere drag. It hangs me up.'

'So that's what you get,' Setters said as they went down to the car. 'Her brother talked like that too until I scared the daylights out of him. You put the fifty-dollar question. Where do they get this hokum from? It isn't film-stuff, not the most of it, nor they don't get it on TV. It just creeps in like an epidemic. It frightens me. They don't care.'

Gently got in, slammed his door. 'I know where it comes from,' he said. 'How it got here is another matter. I'd like the answer to that too.'

'It came with the overspills,' Setters mused.

Gently shook his head. 'No. There's something like it west of Whitehall, but not in Bethnal Green and Stepney.'

'They don't care,' Setters repeated. 'That's what's

different about this lot. They've got that thing about touching something. And they're not quite with you.'

'What's the Listers' address?' Gently asked.

'Now there's someone who cares,' Setters said.

CHAPTER THREE

THEY CHARGED FOUR thousand eight hundred and fifty for the bungalows in Chase Drive and they looked worth about half of that, which is known in some circles as modern architecture. The Lister bungalow was the last in the road, the road being a two-hundred yard cul-de-sac. There were similar bungalows on each side of the road and this one at the bottom, backing straight on the Chase. The Chase at this spot had thirty-year pines with a screen of birches in front of them. The leaves of the birches had turned pale yellow. They trembled. They caught the last of the afternoon sun. The bungalow in front of them was composed of units with flat, shed-like roofs, and was built of glass and varnished wood and painted wood and a little brick. It had a semicircular concrete driveway and the driveway had no gates. In the arc of the driveway was a goldfish pool and a rockery and a small grass plot. There was a sign staked in the grass plot, a varnished section of a tree trunk. It said Treeways. To the right of the driveway was a tradesman's entrance with an iron gate.

'She's all right. Got money,' Setters was saying as they parked. 'Lister was one of the architects here. Coronary occlusion, about a year ago. But he left her well-off, it's all tied up in these houses. She's got a couple of younger kids. Good-looking. Probably marry again.'

'Living alone?' Gently asked.

'Till last week,' Setters replied. 'She's got her mother here now to tide her over for a bit.'

They left the car on the road and walked up the driveway. The main door was plain wood painted white and had an iron bell-pull. It rang some chimes. An elderly woman came. She looked sharply at Gently. Setters addressed her as Mrs Clarkson and did his introduction again.

'Jennifer's dressing,' said Mrs Clarkson. 'You'd better come in, and I'll tell her. But I hope you're not going to be here for long. I'm fetching the children from school shortly.'

'Not for long,' Gently said. 'We could come back tomorrow.'

'It isn't that, but she really isn't fit to talk to people,' said Mrs Clarkson.

She ushered them in through a square hall with a polished parquet floor and into a three-sided, slant-ceilinged room of which the fourth side was a glassed-in veranda. She left them. Setters sat down. Gently moved about the room. The slant-ceiling gave it spaciousness. The furniture was unpolished in a grey-toned wood. The upholstery of the furniture was in off-white and lemon and the carpet was off-white with flecks of black.

The walls were papered in a trellis design. There was a piano. There was a record player.

'What makes a kid from a home like this run riot?' Setters inquired. 'I wish I'd been a kid here. I wish I owned a place like it.'

'When did Lister leave school?' Gently asked.

'That's a point,' Setters said. 'It'd be a year ago, wouldn't it, about the time his old man went. Since when he's been working as a plumber's mate for the firm his father was connected with. Starting at the bottom, more than likely. Not a question of money here.'

'Did Elton work for that firm?' Gently asked.

'Yes,' Setters said. 'Hailey and Lincon's. They're a local firm here in Latchford. They brought in Lister for the overspill project.'

The door from the hall opened. Mrs Lister came in. She was a woman above middle height with a slender waist and wide hips. She had straight-cut gold-brown hair and green eyes and wide cheekbones and under the eyes were blued patches, and the cheeks were pale and a little sagged. She wore a charcoal dress with a bushed skirt. It had a belt. She wore a thin gold chain. She came forward.

'You wanted to see me again?' she asked. She held her hand out to Gently.

'Just a recapitulation,' Gently said. 'I'm fresh here, and it always helps.'

'I want to help you,' said Mrs Lister. 'I keep thinking I haven't helped enough. If Les had been here . . .' She stopped. 'I want to help you all I can,' she said.

She sat down on a wing armchair, crossing her calves

and swinging them slantwise. She laid her hands in her lap. She made a small, hesitant smile for them.

'I keep hoping it was an accident after all,' she said. 'I don't want to know any more than that. It's bad enough that Johnny is dead. I don't think I could bear it if it's something else.'

Gently nodded. 'Life can be unkind.'

'Yes.' She smiled again. 'Yes.'

'And the worst of it is we have to find him,' he said.

'I understand that,' she said. 'I'm simply selfish.'

'How did it start?' he asked. 'All this business. The motorcycling, the slang.'

'I honestly don't know,' Mrs Lister said. 'And yet I do. It happened after Les went.'

'You think that was the cause of it?' Gently asked.

'I feel it had something to do with it,' she said, 'You see, up till that time Johnny was enthusiastic about his career. But Les going upset him terribly. I think there must have been a connection.'

'What was his career to have been?' Gently asked.

'Building and contracting,' she said. 'Les wanted him to be an architect, but Johnny didn't have the same talent for it. It was the practical side that Johnny was good at. Not just using his hands, but organization. So Les said all right, he'd better not waste time at college, and Johnny went straight into Hailey and Lincon's. Which is what he wanted to do.'

'Was he happy there?' Gently asked.

'I thought he was,' Mrs Lister said. 'He used to be talking about it always. And he went to evening classes in Castlebridge.'

'Is that how he came to have a motorcycle?'

'Yes,' she said. 'That was mostly the reason. He had a scooter on his sixteenth birthday, but Castlebridge is twenty-five miles from here.'

'And then what happened?' Gently asked.

'Well, he seemed to lose interest,' Mrs Lister said. 'He dropped the classes. He dropped a lot of his old friends. He became moody and secretive, bored when he was at home. I thought perhaps there was a girl in it. I tried to get him to confide in me. Then there was this awful slang and the passion for jazz records, and the silly clothes he used to wear. I kept hoping it was simply a phase. He wouldn't talk to me about it.'

'He made other friends, didn't he?'

'Yes,' she said. 'though not the sort I approved of. He brought them home once or twice, but he soon stopped doing that. I'm to blame I suppose. I ought to have concealed what I thought of them. But I couldn't help it. They were terrible. I don't think some of them ever washed. And there they sat, in his room, playing jazz records and smoking. Till the small hours, sometimes. I had to say something.'

'Do you remember who they were?' Gently asked.

'I'm not sure I knew their names,' she said. 'But I remember the Elton boy coming. And Elton's sister. And Dicky Deeming.'

'Jack Salmon. Frankie Knights.'

'No,' she said, 'I don't remember. Only Dicky. I thought that Dicky was old enough to have known better. But he's a writer, of course, so he might have been slumming after material.' She made a face. 'If you can call this bungalow a slum,' she added.

'How old is Deeming then?'

'Oh, thirty-ish,' said Mrs Lister. 'He looks younger because he's boyish, short hair and that. He writes for the little reviews, I'm told, and does book notices and things. He's our only local author. That's why I remember him.'

'And Johnny was specially friendly with him?'

'Oh, quite infatuated,' she said. 'For a time, you know. A spell of teenage hero-worship. Dicky was what Johnny wanted to be. Cool, I think is the term they use. A rebel against all convention, a jazz expert and etcetera. For a time he was always around with Dicky. Then Dicky faded out again.'

'Was there any reason for that?' Gently asked.

'I'm not sure,' said Mrs Lister. 'It was around that time, or soon after, that he fell so heavily for Betty Turner. Poor girl. She little knew how it would end, her romance with Johnny. But I think she may have displaced Dicky. I remember thinking so at the time.'

'He was genuinely in love with her, was he?'

Mrs Lister nodded several times. 'He was like his father. Fell with a bang. Very like his father, was Johnny.'

'Did you approve of Betty Turner?'

'I didn't disapprove,' she said. 'I wouldn't have picked her, she's a sad little trollop. But I thought she was a healthier influence than Dicky. If she'd loved Johnny too.'

'She didn't love him?' Gently said.

'No,' said Mrs Lister, 'she didn't. It was just a crush on her side.'

Setters shifted in his chair. 'They were engaged, weren't they?' he said.

'Yes,' she said. 'They were engaged. But it wasn't serious with Betty. If you want my frank opinion they wouldn't have lasted for much longer. She was very pettish just lately. Johnny was much concerned, poor child.'

'Was Elton the trouble?' Gently asked.

'He may have been,' said Mrs Lister. 'I know she used to be fond of Elton and sometimes she teased Johnny about him. I'm not sure. She was pettish and listless. She'd just grown tired of Johnny, I think.'

Gently sat silent for some moments. Mrs Lister was biting her lip. The wing of the armchair shaded her face, her eyes were hooded but staring fixedly. Now the sun had gone in. The light in the room was greyer.

'I've seen your statement,' Gently said, 'about what happened last Tuesday. But I'd like you to go through it again, just in case there's anything you forgot.'

She shuddered. 'I've told you everything,' she said.

'I'd be grateful,' he said, 'if you'd face it.'

She nodded weakly. 'I know I must. You're very kind. I'll try.'

'First,' he said, 'did it differ in any way from your usual Tuesday programme?'

She thought a little. 'I don't think so,' she said. 'I can't remember anything different.'

'You got your youngsters up, did you, got the breakfast and so forth?'

'Mrs Jillings got the breakfast,' she said. 'Mrs Jillings is my daily.'

'Then did you all have breakfast together?'

She shook her head. 'Johnny had his first. He had to be at the site at eight. He was working on the Ford Road project.'

'Did Johnny seem much as usual?'

'Oh, yes,' she said. 'What I saw of him. Except perhaps he was a little short with me. But I'd been used to that, lately. He rang Betty.'

'What about?'

'I don't know. I didn't listen,' she said. 'I thought he was arranging about the evening, you know, the jazz thing in Castlebridge. He used to go there every Tuesday.'

'Did he usually ring her about it?'

'I don't remember,' she said. 'He used to ring Betty a lot.'

'So then you saw him off, did you?'

'I saw him get his bike out,' she said. 'I was dressing Jean in the kiddies' bedroom. I gave him a wave but he didn't see me. Then, well, it was much as always. I drove the kiddies to school. Mrs Jillings did the ironing while I prepared the things for lunch. Then I drove down to town, did some shopping, went to Leonard's for coffee. It can't be of importance. Only to me, that is.'

'Johnny came home to lunch, did he?'

'Yes,' she said, 'at about twenty to one.'

'Was that his usual time for lunch?'

'Oh yes,' she said. 'They leave off at twelve-thirty.'

'Was there anything you noticed at lunch?'

'He was quiet,' she said. 'He had nothing to say. And usually he read the lunchtime paper. I thought he was brooding about Betty. I tried to talk to him about it. I could have helped him, I know. I'd give anything now.' She stopped. 'He snapped at me,' she said.

'What made you think he was brooding over Betty?'

She paused. 'Woman's intuition,' she said. 'But no, that's not quite true, really. I'd seen him worrying over her before. I watched him the more because he'd gone so far from me. I sometimes knew what he was thinking. Poor Johnny. Poor Johnny. But all the time I was with him really.'

'So you'd begun to lose him,' Gently said, 'when you lost your husband.'

She nodded silently. Her hand lifted and fell again in her lap.

'It's been all one tragedy.'

'All one,' she said.

'These kids,' Setters said. He wrung his hands, making the joints crack.

'Was there anything else about lunch?' Gently asked.

She was on the point of shaking her head. She changed her mind. 'One thing,' she said, 'since you want to know every detail. He went to his room when he came in. Before he washed or did anything. I thought perhaps he'd gone to fetch something, but he was carrying nothing when he came out.'

'Did he take something in there?'

'No,' she said, 'he'd nothing with him. Or it was something very small which he carried in his pocket.'

'Have you noticed anything in his room?'

'No, nothing,' she said.

'You've been in there since Tuesday?'

'Once,' she said, 'I went in.'

'Let's go on from after lunch.'

She leant her head on the wing of the chair. 'It was one of those blank afternoons,' she said. 'Nothing happened much at all. After the washing-up I did some mending, Peter's socks, Jean's gym-slip. Then I looked at the TV, but there was nothing on that. So I pottered about in the house till it was time to fetch the kiddies. They'd had their tea and were out playing by the time Johnny got back. He was angrier if anything.'

'Had he been angry before?'

'With me,' she said. 'He'd been angry all day. And now he was angrier. We couldn't exchange a civil word. I was bushed, I felt desperate, I couldn't think what I was going to do about him. I've been miserable. It needed a man. Johnny needed a man to cope with him.'

'Can you remember anything significant he said?'

'It was just angriness,' she said. 'Picking on things, you know, making a tragedy out of nothing. The tea wasn't ready when he wanted it, he couldn't find a clean shirt, Mrs Jillings hadn't pressed his tie, I got in his way in the bathroom. By the time it was over and he'd gone I was practically in tears. I put the kiddies to bed early. Jean came in for a smacking.'

'And you put it down to his anxiety about Betty.'

'Yes,' she said, 'I suppose I did. Betty and everything she stood for.'

'Not just Betty.'

'Betty and the rest. It's all one in my mind,' she said. 'If she'd been a decent sort of girl she wouldn't have led him on so far.'

'Just briefly,' Gently said, 'did anything happen during the evening?'

'I played bridge,' said Mrs Lister. 'The Dawsons came over. I played bridge.'

In the report it said she'd been rung at a quarter to one on the Wednesday morning. Later that day she'd seen the body and identified the motorcycle and some clothes. Her doctor, Setters had said, had given her a strong sedative, but after the initial shock she had declined to use it.

A car pulled in to the driveway.

'That's Mother with the kiddies,' Mrs Lister said.

'One more question,' Gently said, 'then we'll stop being a nuisance to you. What sort of cigarettes did your son smoke?'

Mrs Lister looked puzzled. 'Guards, I think.'

'Did he ever talk of sticks?' Gently asked.

'No,' she said. 'What are sticks?'

'Reefers,' Gently said.

Still Mrs Lister looked puzzled.

'Cigarettes,' he explained, 'with a percentage of marijuana added.'

'Oh,' she said. She flushed slightly. 'That's dope, isn't it?' she said.

Gently nodded. 'That's dope.'

'No,' she said quickly, 'he wouldn't. No.'

'He never mentioned them at all?'

'Never,' she said. 'Not Johnny.'

'You didn't suspect he might be smoking them? They have a strong, heady aroma.'

She hesitated. 'No,' she said. 'Johnny just wouldn't have done it.'

Gently rose. 'Would it very much upset you if we looked through his room?' he said.

Her flush was heightened. 'Very well,' she said. 'You can do that if you want to.'

She rose and led the way out into the hall and down a short passage. They passed a door behind which could be heard the voices of children in expostulation. She checked there but then continued. She opened a door at the end of the passage. It gave into a small bedroom with an enormous window that faced the trees.

'Johnny's room,' she said, catching her breath. She went to the window and stood looking out.

Gently entered. He sniffed delicately. Stale cigarette smoke and newish furnishings. A bedroom suite in unpolished oak, a bedside cabinet, a table. On the table was a record player and a plastic rack stuffed with records. In the top of the cabinet there were books. There was a yellow Penguin on the Buddhist Scriptures. A glass ashtray stood on the cabinet, recently emptied but not washed. A working jacket hung over a chair. Some boots were shoved underneath.

Gently opened the door of the cabinet. It contained magazines, a camera, junk. The dressing-table drawers were crammed with clothes and in the tallboy was clean bedlinen. Setters went over the wardrobe. He had exploring fingers like a pickpocket's. Soon he closed the door noiselessly and gave a small, negative shrug. Shoes, boots were all empty. Nothing was hidden about the bed.

'About how long was Johnny in here at lunchtime on Tuesday?' Gently asked.

'Only a moment,' said Mrs Lister. 'He went straight in and came straight out again.'

Gently went to the doorway, stood looking round the room. He walked across to the record player, snapped the catches, lifted the lid. A record lay on the turntable. He lifted the record. Underneath, wrapped in a serviette, were five unbranded cigarettes. They were clumsily rolled in a greyish paper and made from a coarse brown tobacco. He showed them to Setters.

'Like the others you've seen round here?' he asked.

Setters nodded. He turned one of them over with his nail.

Mrs Lister came forward, stared at the five cigarettes. She was very pale.

'And they're reefers?' she said.

'Yes,' Gently said. 'They're reefers.'

'I can't believe it,' she said. 'Oh God, not Johnny. It's beyond me, I can't believe it. There's no meaning any longer.' She began to laugh hysterically, the tears plunging down her cheeks.

'I'm sorry,' Gently said.

'There's no meaning,' she repeated.

'We'll have to take these,' Gently said. 'We'll perhaps find out who's been pushing them.'

'There's no meaning,' she went on. 'And I'm so tired of it, so tired of it. There's no point in it all. And I'm so tired, so tired.'

Some feet scuffled in the passage. A little boy stood in the doorway. He was six or seven, fair-haired, wearing a school blazer with a huge badge. His eyes were round. His mouth was working. His chubby hands were balled hard. He suddenly ran screaming to Mrs Lister.

'Mummy. Mummy. Mummy. Mummy.'

He buried his face in her stomach. She held him to her with both hands.

'Peter,' she said. 'Peter.'

'Mummy, mummy,' he wailed.

'Peter.'

He twisted round. He stared at Gently. There was a flinching pucker in his face.

'Go away policeman,' he said. 'Go away from my mummy.'

'No, Peter,' said Mrs Lister. 'He's a kind man, Peter.'

'Go away,' Peter said. 'Policeman go away.'

Gently made a sign to Setters.

They took the reefers and went.

'Progress,' Setters said as they drove away from Chase Drive. 'And me the dumbest screw in the force not to have looked for those sticks sooner. Do you think she really didn't know?'

'She didn't know,' Gently said. 'She had suspicions, maybe, but she didn't want to believe them.'

'So he was smoking,' Setters said. 'That alters the picture just a bit. They were both of them smoking. Might have been high when they crashed.'

'Yet he leaves the sticks at home,' Gently said. 'Why was that?'

'Just his home supply,' Setters said. 'You can maybe buy them in Castlebridge.'

'Did you find any at the crash?' Gently asked.

'No,' Setters said. 'But that proves nothing.'

'You'd have thought they'd have had a spare one about them,' Gently said.

Setters rubbed his cheek. 'The girl didn't have any at home,' he said. 'When the medic told us we sent round, but we found nothing there. And it's right, she ought to have had some. She had a case in her bag. It just wouldn't be that chummie Elton whipped those reefers, you think?'

'You've met him,' Gently said.

'Yeah,' Setters said slowly. 'Pass back. He isn't the type. He's next to human. He wouldn't have gone through her bag.'

'I'll want to talk to her,' Gently said. 'Is there a chance of me doing it?'

'I'll ring the blood-house,' Setters said. 'But she hasn't been conscious again since.'

They parked at H.Q. and went through to Setters' office. He rang the hospital. Betty Turner was still in a coma. Gently had spread out the reefers and the serviette on a sheet of paper on Setter's desk. He sat looking at them while Setters phoned, pushing them about with the tip of a pen-holder.

Setters hung up.

'You'll have heard,' he said.

Gently shrugged, put down the pen-holder.

'What do we know about them?' Setters asked.

'They're a common make,' Gently said. 'We've picked up scores of this type in Soho and points west.

They've been a headache for some time. You'd better dust them and send them to Narcotics.'

Setters nodded. 'And the serviette?'

'Dust that too,' Gently said. 'Then put a man on tracing its origin. He can start on the cafés in the Ford Road area.'

'Yes,' Setters said. 'That's probably where Lister got those sticks on the Tuesday morning. He wasn't late home so it'd be in the tea-break, and he wouldn't go far from the site for that.'

'One other thing,' Gently said. 'Suppose you wanted to pull a jeebie. Where's the most likely place to lay hands on one?'

Setters thought about it. 'Try the First and Last café,' he said. 'You'll find it just out of town on the Norwich Road.'

'Is it cool, man?' Gently asked.

'Bloody arctic,' said Setters.

'Like I may make the scene after a meal,' Gently said.

CHAPTER FOUR

AT THE SUN Gently ordered a high tea and while he ate it read the evening paper. Two reporters had been waiting at H.Q. when he first arrived there and after the conference he had given them a short non-committal statement. He had been photographed. The photograph appeared on the front page. It showed him stooping to enter the Rover, on the whole a flattering shot. It was recognizable also. His waitress had recognized it. She now addressed him as Mr Gently and had a conversation about him with another waitress. The manager, who'd known about him all along, nodded to him with superior deference.

Setters looked in again after tea with the results of the print-taking, but the prints on the reefers had been few and partial and those on the serviette were Lister's. He'd sent out Ralphs with the serviette and expected a report from him during the evening. Ralphs had been on the case from the beginning: he was keen not to be dropped now.

'Will you want me with you this evening?' Setters had asked.

Gently had grinned. 'Am I likely to need you?'

'Not in this town you shouldn't,' Setters had replied. 'But you might not be popular where you are going.'

He'd borrowed the paper and gone out looking at it. But only his arm had shown in the picture.

At half-past seven Gently left, after studying a plan of Latchford which hung in the hotel hall. He drove up the High Street, turned right at the top, drove some distance through a residential street. The street ended abruptly. There was open country beyond it. The lights were cut off quite sharply and beyond them was blackness. A little further right was a pull-up backed by a low, dim-lit building, and on the building was a red neon sign which read: First And Last. He drove in and parked between a truck and a small van. Next to the van, parked in a square, were six or seven motorcycles. When he got out from the car he could hear canned jazz music, somebody beating out the rhythm, a girl's voice raised in a squeal. He went over and through the door. Opposite the door was an espresso bar. The building was L-shaped, furnished with tables and chairs, underlit and overheated. He crossed to the bar.

'I'll have a cup of coffee,' he said.

The man at the bar looked like an Italian, he had thin features and a twitch. At a table near the bar a truck-driver was eating. The rest of the tables near the bar were empty. It was round the corner where the noise was coming from. There one could partly see the illuminated bulk of a jukebox.

'I fix you some eats?' the Italian said.

'No,' Gently said. He paid for his coffee.

'Some sandwiches, fruit?' the Italian said.

Gently shrugged, walked away, the Italian watching him.

Round the corner they'd pushed the tables back and were sitting in a group. There were ten youths and six girls and, in the centre, an older man. Most of the youths wore black riding leathers, black sweaters, black boots. The others wore short, patterned jackets, black sweaters, black jeans. The girls wore various sweaters, black jeans, black ballerinas. They all wore ban-the-bomb badges. They sat on chairs and on the floor.

Gently walked up to the group. He stood drinking his coffee. They didn't stop beating out rhythm but all their eyes were fixed on him. One of the girls was Maureen Elton. She squealed something to her neighbour. The jukebox was turned up very loud, it was thumping out New Orleans Blues. The Italian came round the end of the bar, kept making gestures with his head to someone. The eyes that watched Gently didn't have expression, they were just watchful, continuedly.

The jazz stopped, leaving a humming. The Italian went very still. From down by the counter came the clatter of the truck-driver's cutlery. Three of the youths got to their feet, one of them strutted towards Gently. He had a handsome, fresh-complexioned face but with a wide mouth and a receding brow. He stood before Gently, hands on hips. Gently finished his coffee, put down the cup.

'Like what gives?' the youth said.

Gently didn't say anything.

'Like I'm asking you, square,' the youth said.

Gently felt in his pocket for his pipe.

'You want I clue you?' the youth said. 'Like you're dumb or some jazz? We don't go for squares in this scene. Like you're smart you'll blow pronto.'

Gently began filling his pipe.

'Like you're smart,' the youth said.

Gently went on filling his pipe. 'Sidney,' he said, 'you'd better sit down.'

The youth got up on his toes. 'What's that tag again?' he said.

'Sidney Bixley,' Gently said.

'Say it again,' said the youth.

'Sidney Bixley,' Gently said. 'Six months in Brixton for armed assault.'

He finished filling his pipe and lit it.

'So just sit down, Sidney,' he said.

There was a squawk from Maureen Elton. 'He's that screw I was shooting about. The one they've got down from the Smoke. Like he knows about you, Sidney.'

'I don't know that,' Sidney said. He'd fetched his hands off his hips. 'I don't know nothing about screws. Like cocky squares I know about.'

'He'll hang you up,' Maureen said.

'Cocky squares,' Sidney said.

'Like you'd better not flip your lid,' Maureen said.

'I murder squares,' Sidney said.

'Sid,' said the older man, 'keep it cool, man. Do as he says.'

'Like making in here,' Sidney said.

'No, keep it cool,' said the older man.

Gently puffed. He came forward. He pushed Sidney

to one side. Sidney staggered, went falling, got tangled up with a chair. He jumped up and stood swearing. His two followers did nothing. Gently spun a chair back to front. He sat down, looked round him.

'Dicky Deeming?' he said.

The older man gave him a nod. 'You're well clued-in, man,' he said. 'Don't seem to need introductions.'

'I didn't know Lister,' Gently said.

Deeming smiled faintly, said nothing.

'You were all friends of his?' Gently said.

'Yes,' Deeming said. 'We were his friends.'

'But somebody wasn't,' Gently said.

'So you tell us,' Deeming said.

'He was killed,' Gently said.

'Like that's certain, man,' Deeming said.

He was around thirty, tall, with a large, gaunt-cheeked face, light hair cut close, slate eyes, big ears. He wore a white-trimmed black windcheater, black jeans, sandals. He had a hard, large-framed body. It showed well in the windcheater.

'So what's your theory?' Gently said.

'Like why should I have one?' Deeming asked. 'You've talked to Maureen, she says, you know what we think about Johnny. He made it, that's all, he was out there with them. That's crazy, it sends us. Johnny comes very big with us.'

'Yuh, big, he's big with us,' several of them growled.

'He was the mostest, coolest,' said a girl with dark hair.

'And as for this jazz about his being busted,' Deeming said, 'like we've seen enough of screws to know the action they make.'

'You think we're lying to you?' Gently asked.

'Throwing a curve,' Deeming said. 'That's not lying, it's trying it on, hoping it's going to fit some place. You don't like hipsters in Squaresville. You like to put the heat on them. So you make a deal out of Johnny and come pushing us around with it.'

'And like we don't stand for it,' Bixley said, stepping up closer.

'Cool it, Sid,' Deeming said. 'Pitching screws is for squares.'

'He bugs me, this guy does,' said Bixley. 'Me, I could spread him on the wall.'

'Dicky says cool it,' Maureen said. 'So cool it quick, you big ape.'

Gently puffed a few times. 'You know we've spoken to Betty Turner?' he said.

'The screws,' Deeming said, 'don't keep us posted with the news.'

'She confirms that someone rode them off the road that night.'

'Like you could imagine things,' Deeming said. 'With leading questions when you're muzzy.'

'All right,' Gently said. 'So the police are lying their heads off. Lister crashed himself for the kick, and didn't give a damn about his fiancée. And Elton ran away from nothing, because there was nothing to run away from. And there's nobody here who smokes reefers or knows where reefers can be obtained.'

Nobody said anything for a couple of moments. They were all scowling, but they didn't say anything. Bixley was grinning a stupid grin and showing his teeth at

Gently. The Italian had faded behind his counter but he still had his ear cocked. Deeming alone wasn't scowling. He'd got the least bit of a smile.

'It's a kick, smoking,' he said. 'It's a kick, and it touches. Jeebies go for the touches, they don't give a damn for Squaresville. Like I've smoked myself, man, when I was up in the Smoke, and you won't never stop it. If you could've done you would've.'

'Lister,' Gently said, 'had five sticks in his possession.'

Maureen's hand flew to her mouth. Her eyes went to Bixley.

'Like you've answered it, screw,' Bixley said, still grinning with his teeth. 'Like he'd been smoking that night. Wouldn't make him ride good.'

'You were at that jazz session,' Gently said.

'So what does that make?' Bixley said.

'You were where you could see if he was smoking. And what he was smoking,' Gently said.

'Yuh,' Bixley said, 'sure. Like I went there just to watch him. Got my chick along, too, but I was watching Johnny Lister.'

'Which is Anne Wicks?' Gently asked.

'That's my tag,' said the dark girl. 'And it's right what Sid says, we didn't have no time for Johnny.'

'There's sticks about,' said Deeming quietly. 'But like where they come from is nobody's guess. They get passed along from hand to hand, that's how sticks get into the scene.'

'Yuh, that's how,' Bixley said.

'Like you touch your pals for them,' said Deeming.

Gently looked Bixley over. Bixley showed some

more of his teeth. The record said he'd been a gang-member two years ago, in Bethnal. There was nothing against him here, Setters had said, skipping a couple of traffic offences. At times he worked as a casual labourer at one or another of the construction sites.

'You digging me good, screw?' said Bixley.

Gently gave him his slow nod.

'We'd have done you up in Bethnal,' said Bixley. 'That's telling you, screw. We'd have done you up.'

Gently puffed. 'Someone did Lister up.'

It's a bleeding lie,' Bixley said.

'You passed the crash. Yet you didn't see it.'

'So like what if I didn't?' Bixley said.

'Elton saw it, and he stopped. But you didn't,' Gently said.

'Just needle me some more,' Bixley said. 'Just one more jab from you, screw.'

'Sid,' said Deeming, 'take some ice.'

'Like who is telling me?' Bixley asked.

'Take some ice, Sid,' Deeming said. 'And stop behaving like a cornball.'

'This screw is pushing me,' Bixley said.

'Screws,' Deeming said, 'are always pushing. But cool it, man, and cool it good. Don't get hung up over a square.'

'I don't go for pushing,' Bixley said.

'You listen to Dicky,' Deeming said.

He got up. He stretched himself. He looked a giant beside Bixley. He patted Bixley on the shoulder, gave him a lazy sort of smile.

'Go and drop a nickel,' he said, 'let's make with the music again.'

'Crazy,' Maureen Elton said. 'You drop the nickel in, Sid.'

'I don't get pushed,' Bixley said.

'We all get pushed,' Deeming said. 'But you do the cool thing, Sid. Like keep it down and make with the music.'

He started Bixley towards the jukebox. Bixley hung on for a moment, then he went. When he'd set the jukebox thumping he stood beside it looking sulky. Deeming turned back to Gently.

'Like we could talk it up,' he said. 'Over in my pad if that suits you. We could talk it up there.'

'We could talk what up?' Gently asked.

Deeming grinned. 'The scene,' he said. 'What a screw should know about it. The real jazz. The cool thing.'

'I might not get that,' Gently said.

'Sure, you'll get it,' Deeming said. 'Then you'll be all clued-in. Like you're missing something now.'

He signalled the Italian to come over.

'Pack us a feed-bag, Tony,' he said. 'I've got a screw coming to supper, so make it crazy, make it wild.'

Eastgate Street was the old town where it merged into the new, a crooked backstreet slanting into one of the overspill highways. It didn't show many lights, a lot of the buildings were warehouses, but at the further end were new buildings, office blocks, a filling station. Deeming had rooms over one of the warehouses. They were behind the filling station and looked over it to an overspill neighbourhood. The approach from the street was down a side lane fenced from the filling station with square-mesh netting, then through a door and down an unlit passage to some bare stairs and a landing. Off the landing were two doors, one of them lettered 'W.C.', the other opening into two rooms which were the extent of the accommodation. Deeming had struck matches on the way up but inside the second door there was a light switch.

'What they'd call in the Village a cold-water walk-up pad,' he said. 'Like it's *de rigueur* with the beatniks, but jeebies aren't so hung up.'

'You've lived in America, then?' Gently asked.

'I had two years there,' Deeming said. 'Me, I'm a nowhere sort of cat, but I came from Sidney in the first place. But like I couldn't groove in that scene and I kept on kicking along eastwards. I went up the islands and across to 'Frisco, then coast-to-coast, then away here. Like I was searching for something, screw, and maybe I've found it, maybe I haven't.'

He plugged in an electric stove, waved his hand to a chair. Then he fetched a plate from a cupboard and unpacked Tony's sandwiches on to it. The room was large with a high ceiling and had probably been an office once. The walls were painted a yellowing cream and the woodwork brown, which was beginning to blister. The wood floor was naked, was kept swept but not washed. The furniture comprised six bedroom chairs, two tables, two cupboards, a dresser and a bench. At one end was a sink and an old gas-cooker. The windows didn't have curtains. There was an obsolete typewriter on one of the tables, stacks of paper, typed MS. On the other table was a record player, a record case, a guitar. On the floor and everywhere there were books in piles. Most of the books were new, had review slips sticking out of them.

From the other cupboard Deeming took two balloon glasses and a bottle of Spanish Sauternes. He drew the cork, poured into the glasses, put the plate of sandwiches on the table between them. Then he switched on the player, put a record on the turntable. He turned it down very low. It was Grieg's piano concerto. He sat down opposite Gently.

'Like you shouldn't have kept pressuring Bixley,' he said. 'That guy couldn't have busted off Lister, and he flips his lid in two shakes.'

Gently said nothing. He sipped the Sauternes. Deeming sipped his too.

'He's a hothead,' Deeming continued. 'We all know about that. He was on a jail kick for pitching. Like it's easy to see how. But you know something,' Deeming asked, 'something that isn't quite so obvious? We've cooled him down since he's been with us, and like he isn't pushed, he stays cool. And then there's nothing wrong with that guy. He keeps it down, he's a cool jeebie. So don't go pressuring him unless you have to. We don't like him ribbed into flipping his lid.'

He looked level with his slate eyes, reached for a sandwich and began to eat.

'We don't go for flipping lids at all,' he said. It's too square, man. It's torrid.'

Gently nodded, kept sipping. 'Where were you on Tuesday?' he asked.

Deeming finished chewing his sandwich. 'Up at Tony's,' he said. 'Not busting off Lister.'

'Have you a bike?' Gently asked.

'Sure,' Deeming said, 'the mostest going. I ride a Bonneville with all the action, sank a year's loot in it. But man, it hasn't a scratch on it, nor any notches on the butt. And Johnny wasn't bust, you know. Let's talk up things fundamental.'

'Murder,' Gently said, 'is fundamental with me.'

'You like salami and garlic?' Deeming said. 'Latch on to one of Tony's sandwiches.'

Gently latched on to a sandwich. The Grieg went on thumping and tinkling.

'Now the way you see this action,' Deeming said, 'is delinquent kids kicking it up. The war generation, you say, cocking the stale old snook at their elders. They've got a fresh curve, maybe, but it's the old complaint they're hung up with. They want to poke the old man's snot. They want to act themselves big. That's the way you see this action, and man, you're not seeing it so good.'

'I can see it being lawless,' Gently said.

'You'll never change that,' Deeming said. 'That's a perpetual factor in civilization where every law is an experiment.'

'An experiment backed by consent,' Gently said.

'But still an experiment,' Deeming said. 'And backed by the consent of its generation, not by the generation that follows. With them the experiment continues, or as you say, they are lawless. And then the laws become modified by a new act of consent. Today they hang you for a shilling, tomorrow they lock up the hangman. Like you're merely stating the obvious by calling any man lawless.'

'Yet people suffer because of it,' Gently said.

'Sure,' Deeming said. 'I'm with you there.'

'And it has to be checked,' Gently said. 'Or the next stage is anarchy.'

'I'm still with you,' Deeming said. 'But that's the process, for better or worse. Society acts, the individual reacts, there's a percentage of suffering, and there's modification.'

'And there's individual responsibility,' said Gently.

'There,' said Deeming, 'is the ground of contention.'

He refilled the glasses, took a long sip from his. From the player came a long trumpet-call melting into the note of a single instrument. Deeming paused, listening to it. He caught Gently's eye, smiling.

'Like I've made a point,' he said. 'Don't knock this action for kicking the law. They kick it in Sunday school circles and all over Squaresville in general. But maybe it gets kicked less with us, I wouldn't know, I don't see the figures. But the cool thing, screw, is to keep it down. We aim not to get hung up with the squares.'

'You're still cocking a snook at them,' Gently said.

'Sure,' Deeming said. 'But let's get on from there. Because cocking a snook is all the squares see of it, and it's the way it's cocked that really matters. Like there's a change they haven't noticed. Like it isn't just growing pains any longer. Like it's a historic reaction going on against a life direction that's played itself out. You dig it, man, what I'm giving you?'

Gently nodded. 'I think I do.'

'Crazy,' Deeming said. 'I figured you were smarter than some of these screws. Like there's a revolution going on, not just in Russia but everywhere. In Russia and China it's a mass revolution, but in the West it's individual. Like we're dragged to death with this society and its nowhere aims and its chromium shop-front. We just don't go for it, we're opting out, we're leaving it be to hang itself up. We want to live it real, man, to touch the real. We're sick and tired of the illusion. Christ-ish jazz, we're tired of that, and piling loot, and conning our neighbour. You can knock Russia for being a police state, but hell, it gives a Russian some real to live with.'

'But you're no Communist,' Gently said.

'Like I told you, we're personal with ours,' Deeming said. 'The Communist deal makes the state a family, but like in the West we're ashamed of our family. So we kick it, we're individual. We go for it way out with the birds. That's making the touch on a personal basis, keeping it down with having relations. You dig relations? It's overvaluing someone, making yourself too vulnerable. When I feel I might be having a relation I pull up my stakes and get easting again.'

'That way,' Gently said, 'you'll finish up under a Bo tree.'

Deeming nodded. 'You're with me, screw. It might be a Bo tree at that. Like keep it down in every way and go for the final kick in the book. I sometimes think I'll make that scene. I'm only part way out, yet.'

'With a begging bowl?' Gently asked.

'Right,' Deeming said. 'A good Buddhist must beg.'

'If all the world were good Buddhists,' Gently said, 'who would fill the bowls for them?'

Deeming chuckled. 'Like you've put a finger on it,' he said. 'But all religions are contradictory, and the Buddhist jazz is the least so. I don't know. I go some way with it. It's got a logic that sends me. The Christers counter fear with faith, the Buddhists stare it in the eyeballs.'

'It asks you to be ahuman,' Gently said.

'Don't all religions?' Deeming asked.

The Grieg thundered to a close. Deeming rose, turned over the record. The muted second movement began, a gentle, nostalgic meditation. Deeming sat down and ate a sandwich, sat listening, his *yes* beyond Gently. Gently also ate another sandwich. A motorbike blasted by on the highway.

'I'm sorting it out,' Deeming said, 'I'm writing a novel, sorting it out. Like it was time it made the record, what I've been giving the jeebies here.'

'I thought it had been done,' said Gently. 'By Kerouac.'

'Kerouac,' said Deeming, 'like he's John the Baptist. But I'm way out further than Kerouac was. I picked it up where Kerouac dropped it.'

He ate and drank some more.

'I'll try to give it to you,' he said. 'You're the only screw I could ever talk to, so I'll lay it on the line for you. Now the big jazz is touching the real – you dig me, man, touching the real?'

Gently nodded slowly. 'Breaking through the illusion to the essence,' he said.

'Right,' Deeming said, 'that's how a square would define touching. You make some action and grab a kick and like it's wild enough, you're touching. Now keep with me. Did you ever have a shock off a D.C. system?'

'Once,' Gently admitted. 'It used to be D.C. in my rooms.'

'It was like this, wasn't it,' said Deeming. 'First it was like your fingers exploded. Then it was like them being burned. Then they exploded again when you broke contact.'

'That's roughly it,' Gently said.

'Take another instance,' Deeming said. 'You've turned a corner in a garden. You see a flower, a crazy flower; it sends you, looking at this flower. Now when you first see it you get that explosion, it hits you smack down to your bowels. Then it burns you, you aren't with it, you just keep looking and thinking at it. Then, when you find you've lost touch, you turn away, and it hits you again. Only the first bang is the big one, like it is with the D.C. shock. Are you along?'

Gently nodded.

'Take another instance,' Deeming said. 'You're coming through a big belt of mountains. All day you've had these peaks around you, you're getting dragged by so many peaks. Then you come over a pass and see a great plain beneath you, and the peaks are standing over the plain, and the plain is wide under the peaks. And that hits you, the plain and the peaks, coming together like that, though you're dragged with the peaks and the plain is just nothing. But where they meet like that it pulls you up and sends you. You get the on-off-on like I've just been giving you.'

Gently nodded.

'Take the instance right here,' Deeming said. 'Go and dig one of these neighbourhoods with all its contemporary style action. It's nowhere, man. It's a drag. Like you'd throw stones at the windows. Then dig it here, where it joins the old town, and you get the on-off-on again. Like it's the same with the old town where it doesn't meet the new.'

'Is that the reason,' Gently asked, 'why you're living just here?'

'Too right it is,' Deeming said. 'I picked this spot out of a million. Like it doesn't come older than this anywhere in Europe. The Abos were mining flints here, this was big Abo country. Then the Romans, then the kings, then the Danes and that jazz. And Tom Paine, you dig him? Like I wanted to see his country. Like the States would have been South Canada if it hadn't been for Tom Paine. And right here, man, you've got the collision, where that wire fence runs. And that's the jazz I'm trying to sound: that the real is timeless, and it's at the borders. Like you want to keep touching you have to live along the borders.'

He smiled at Gently, lifted a finger.

'Listen to this,' he said.

The Grieg had swirled into a crescendo, was fading a moment into soft strings. Then a single flute sounded, filling in a trill like cascaded water, spreading out and losing itself in the heavy rocks of the cellos. Some bars later the piano caught it and made it a crashing torrent, then it lost itself in a thousand echoes of its brief, perfect poignancy.

'Like that,' Deeming said, 'that was Grieg touching the real. You wanted it back, but he wouldn't give it to you. He kept it timeless, along the borders.'

'And Lister,' said Gently, 'was along the borders when he rode over the verge?'

'Crazy,' said Deeming. 'You're getting it, man. Like I didn't think I could put it over.'

Gently put down his glass, watched it, let the Grieg clamour its finale. The gear clicked, raised the pick-up, dropped it on its stud and killed the motor.

'And Betty Turner,' he said. 'Lister would ignore her, of course.'

'He'd forget her,' Deeming said. 'He wouldn't remember she was with him.'

'Too bad,' Gently said.

'Sure, too bad,' said Deeming. 'But that's the way of it, screw. You're kidding yourself if you think it wasn't.'

'I don't think I'm kidded,' Gently said.

'A square self-kidded,' said Deeming. 'Man, we'll put this bottle out of its misery, then I'll make with something really cool.'

'Not for me,' Gently said.

'Come off it, screw,' said Deeming, grinning.

CHAPTER FIVE

SETTERS WAS BACK at the hotel at breakfast-time carrying a worn, empty-gutted briefcase, and he was shown into the dining-room where Gently was still eating breakfast.

'We traced the serviette,' he said, unbuckling the briefcase on his knee. 'I had Ralphs type his report so you could have it first thing. He ran the serviette down in the Kummin Kafe, in the neighbourhood centre in Dane's Green. That's half a mile from Ford Road but only a step from Spalding and Skinner's. The Turner girl worked there. We think he met her in the Kummin Kafe.'

Gently grunted, not overpleased to be disturbed so early. But Setters was ferreting in the briefcase and eventually handed across the report.

'The man at the café, name of Greenstone, remembered Lister from the published photograph. Said he was regular there at the tea-break and used to meet a girl there.'

'Did he remember the girl?' Gently asked.

'Not to be positive,' Setters said. 'They get a lot of

them in there from the offices, there's more girls than men work there. But Ralphs got some other stuff from him, as you'll see in the report. It looks as though the sticks were passed to the girl and then she passed them on to Lister.'

Gently hung the sheet over his teapot, went on lading some toast with marmalade. He hadn't slept any too well, he'd caught a headache from Deeming's Sauternes. Then, arriving downstairs, he'd seen with surprise that his interview with Deeming had 'made' a morning paper. More, it was Deeming himself who had reported it and whose name was given in the byline.

SUPT. GENTLY'S NIGHT OUT
WITH THE JEEBIES

For a little review contributor, Deeming had a nice journalistic touch. The story that followed was slightly mocking, showed Gently as a bumbling father-figure: not explicitly, of course, but by a number of subtle, overt touches. The piece had also been made a vehicle to give some of Deeming's ideas an airing. He must have wasted no time on the effort, but gone at his typewriter the moment Gently left.

'I saw the write-up,' Setters said, his glance moving to Gently's paper. 'I should have warned you about Dicky Deeming; he's never slow to place a story.'

'I'm used to it,' Gently grunted.

'But I should have warned you,' Setters said. 'The way he writes it he was stringing you along, he asked you up to clinch his story.'

'What else did Ralphs get?' Gently asked.

'That was most of it,' Setters said. 'The rest is down there in the report. I'd say that the girl didn't want to pass the sticks.'

Gently ate and read. The report was lengthy and detailed. Ralphs had started near the Ford Road site and worked conscientiously back into the town. He came to the Kummin Kafe, where the serviette was matched: there'd been a container of them on the counter near a plastic sandwich-case. Ralphs had seen Greenstone in a private room, had got an account from him of the Tuesday tea-break. As usual, Greenstone had been rushed off his feet, so he hadn't had much leisure to observe specific goings-on. Yes, there were some girls from Spalding and Skinner's, and also from a dozen other offices; some fellows, too, clerks and assistants, he didn't particularly remember whom. He remembered Lister, however, because he came in regularly, and then his picture had been in the paper when 'all this was going on'. Lister had been wearing overalls with a jacket thrown over them, he'd gone straight to a corner table where a girl was sitting with a fellow. The fellow had also been wearing overalls. Greenstone thought he'd left when Lister arrived. Lister remained some minutes talking to the girl, and Greenstone's impression was that there was some sort of an argument. Anyway, Lister took something from a tub-bag which was stood on the table, and the girl said: 'No Johnny, they're mine,' or something similar. Later Lister had bought a cup of tea and had taken a serviette from the container, and that was all Greenstone had noticed. He didn't see if they left together. Ralphs had shown him a photograph of Elton and asked him if that was the other fellow. Greenstone wasn't certain, nor could he identify a photograph of Betty Turner. Why was he certain it was the Tuesday? There was a delivery from Mowbray's, the pie people. Greenstone had been putting pies in the case when Lister bought his tea and took the serviette.

Gently checked through it twice before handing it back to Setters.

'You think it was Elton?' Setters asked. 'Would he be the one who passed her the reefers?'

Gently shrugged. 'She seemed only just to have got them,' he said. 'A pity Greenstone can't remember what went on between her and the other fellow.'

'If it was Elton,' Setters said, 'it helps the way I've been seeing it. The sticks may or may not come into it, but that meeting and argument are significant. Let's say that Elton went to meet her there, that he knows she's cooling off from Lister. He tries to talk her round to ditching Lister and maybe into going with him, Elton, to the jazz session. But Betty won't have it, she's still sticking to Lister, then Lister arrives and Elton goes off in a paddy. Lister doesn't like it either, he has an argument about it with Betty, and in the end he grabs her sticks – maybe because she should have had some for him. That way we've got some background to what happened outside the milk bar in Castlebridge. Elton is bitter, he tries to quarrel with Lister, and later he rides him off the road.'

'It hangs together,' Gently admitted. 'But it might have been two other people in the café.'

'I don't think so,' Setters said. 'It fits together too neatly. We wanted a bit more to build on than just that incident outside the milk bar, and this gives it to us. We'll get the truth of it when the girl can talk again.'

'If she'll talk about it,' Gently said. 'She sounded as though she wanted to protect Elton.'

'She'll see it differently,' Setters said, 'when I can show her the case against Elton.'

Gently poured a last cup, began to stoke his pipe.

'Any news about Elton come in?' he asked.

'No,' Setters said, frowning. 'It's beginning to bother me, that is. He's been adrift for nearly a week now, and it's not as though he was a professional. I rang London like you told me and had another talk with them this morning. They've had a check-up in Bethnal, but Elton's not been seen there. A kid on the run with no money, I don't like that one little bit.'

'Meaning,' Gently said.

'Well . . .' Setters opened his hands. 'You get hunches that don't add up. I keep starting to think that Elton's dead.'

'Mmn.' Gently lit the pipe. He broke the match into a tray.

It doesn't add up,' Setters repeated. 'But I can't get the idea out of my head. If I'm right, then it's suicide, and that could hardly go undiscovered. I don't know, I'm a pushover for hunches. But I wish we could find that kid.'

'You've checked on his pals?' Gently asked.

'Yes,' Setters said. 'We've checked twice over. Latchford's a small place, it's isolated. I'll swear on oath that he's not in Latchford.'

'How about outside it?' Gently asked.

'Take a look at the map,' Setters said. 'It's open country for ten miles round, except the Chase, which the rangers watch. The rest we've tackled, every cottage and farmyard – and there's precious few of either. No, he's out of the Latchford area. Unless he's pushing up daisies somewhere.'

'He'll turn up,' Gently said. He pushed back his chair, rose, and stretched. 'I think I'll talk to that milk bar,' he said. 'What was the name and address again?'

'The Ten Spot Milk Bar,' Setters said. 'In Prince's Road. Not far from the station.'

'In the meantime,' Gently said, 'we might take a search warrant to Elton's house. His sister has probably cleaned up the traces, but we can look. There'll be no harm in that.'

He drove out of the Sun yard, where the stagecoaches had wheeled in, across the bridge over the River Latch and past a dull straggle of flint-built dwellings. A fingerpost pointed to Castlebridge, twenty-four miles, then he was out on the wide brecks with a reef of the Chase spreading in from the right.

It was a heavy October day, the sun hazy in a white sky. He swept by still-leaved, wiry birches, and later past coppery oaks and yellow horse-chestnuts. At Oldmarket, thirteen miles from Latchford, a string of race-horses trotted on the heath. Their coats looked liquid in the soft-filtered sun and two of their riders were wearing pink and blue shirts. Through the town the grandstands appeared on the right, heavy-shadowed, lonely, far-distant from the road. A few miles further on lay a military aerodrome with planes standing shaggy in dew-drenched covers.

Castlebridge was coming to life as he drove through the out-streets. Vans were busy, there were reckless droves of starved undergraduates on bicycles. Buses, filled with gown workers, were sedately threading their way to the centre, and people were hurrying along the street which led from the station. Gently swung into Prince's Road, drove slowly down it. It was a wide road lined with a mixture of residential and commercial properties. He noticed a Victorian Gothic church, a red-brick Veterinary Institute, a garage and a tyre-store interspersed among rooming houses and small hotels. The Ten Spot Milk Bar was nearer the town end of the road. It lay between a surplus store on one side and a furniture store on the other. Across the road from it was a free car park which stretched over to a street on the far side. Gently drove into it and parked, got out, crossed the street.

He paused to take in the front of the milk bar, which was only then opening. It ranged the width of two shop-fronts and consisted of down-to-the-pavement windows. The windows were framed with thin fluted pillars that spread into arches at the top and the glass was misted inside so that the lights behind it shone through blurredly. Over the windows was a neon name-sign and a large painted ten of spades card. In the windows hung plastic menu-holders and neon signs reading 'snacks', 'lunches'. There was also a large poster advertising a 'Weekly Jazz Stampede', given alternately by the Castle Cats and the Academic City Stompers.

He went in.

Behind the windows was the usual plastic-and-chromium bar, high stools, range of counters, section of tables for served meals. A pale blonde woman in a pink overall-coat was wiping the bar with a dishcloth. A coffee machine was steaming near her and charging the air with warm coffee smell.

'Yays?' she said to Gently.

'Is the boss in?' Gently asked.

'Are you a traveller?' said the pale blonde.

'In a manner of speaking,' Gently said.

The pale blonde looked him over, didn't seem to like him much. She flicked the dishcloth over the chrome, dropped it in a bowl under the counter.

'Down there,' she said. 'Mr Leach is in the cellar.'

'Thank you,' Gently said.

The pale blonde made no comment.

What she had indicated was a gloomy stair-entrance under a small mezzanine floor at the end of the bar: from which, however, carpeted steps descended, and over which was an illuminated arrow. Gently went down the steps. They turned left at a half-landing. They gave into a long, windowless room lit at present by a single bulb at the other end. Along the walls some chairs were stacked and in a corner a few tables. The floor at the sides and back was carpeted but was polished wood in the centre and at the lit end. There, under the bulb, stood an orchestra dais, painted black with silver trimmings. A man was sitting on the orchestra dais. He had some boxes of chocolates on the rostrum beside him. One of the boxes was open and had apparently been spilt: the man was dusting the spilt chocolates and carefully replacing them. He heard Gently and came to his feet.

'You,' he said. 'What do you want down here?'

'Are you Mr Leach?' Gently asked.

'Yeah,' the man said, 'Joe Leach. So what?'

'I want to talk to you,' Gently said. 'About last Tuesday evening.'

The man stood scowling at him, one of the chocolates in his hand. He was around fifty, about five-eight, stockily built with powerful shoulders. He had a round head and a short neck and the thickened nose of an ex-boxer. His mouth was small but thick-lipped. His eyes were muddy-coloured and squinting. He wore a long jacket in silver grey with silver streaks woven into it, a cream shirt with embossed stars and a pale blue bow-tie. His trousers were pale blue to match the tie. His shoes were white-and-tan and had pointed toes.

'What are you?' he said. 'Another screw, are you?'

Gently mentioned his credentials.

'Yeah,' said Leach. 'I thought you was one. Funny that, how you can tell a screw.' He put the chocolate back in the box, nudging it along into place. He picked up another one and examined it. 'So what are you after now?' he said.

'I told you,' Gently said. 'I want to talk about Tuesday evening.'

'You know about it,' Leach said. 'A couple of hours I was with the screws.'

'We know some more now,' Gently said.

Leach polished the chocolate. 'What?' he said.

'Just a few more details,' Gently said. 'So I thought I'd pay you another visit.'

He went up the steps on to the dais and sat down on a low rostrum beside Leach. Leach kept on his feet, polishing the chocolate. Then he niched that one back into place, too.

'Prizes,' he said. 'Spot prizes. They go down big, a box of chocolates.'

'You had an accident with that box?' Gently asked.

'Yeah,' Leach said. 'I dropped the bleeder. Lucky none of the chocs were bust. What more do I have to tell you about Tuesday?'

'Did you know Lister by sight?' Gently asked.

'I'd seen him around here,' Leach said.

'Deeming, Elton?' Gently said. 'Salmon, Knights, Sidney Bixley?'

'I knew Elton,' Leach said. 'Maybe the others, I wouldn't know.'

'Deeming's about thirty,' Gently said.

'So he don't come here,' Leach said. 'They're all of them youngsters that come to the jazz nights, not above twenty, any one of them.'

'Bixley's twenty-two,' Gently said. 'About your build, good-looking, wide mouth.'

'We get above a hundred here on a jazz night. I can't remember all that lot, can I?' Leach said.

'But you remember Lister and Elton,' Gently said.

'Do me a favour,' Leach said, 'will you? I've had those two crammed down my throat, I ain't never likely to forget them. The screws describe them. They show me photographs. They make it like a crime if I don't know them. Maybe I'd remember some of the others if you kept telling me who they were.'

He grabbed up some chocolates, neglected to polish them, shoved them roughly into the box.

'Did you see them together,' Gently asked, 'any time during the evening?'

'I run this show,' Leach said. 'Do you think I've got time to see who's with who?'

'Did you?' Gently asked.

Leach leaned on the rostrum. 'Whose been talking?' he said.

'People do talk,' Gently said. 'Did you see Lister and Elton together?'

Leach kept leaning. He was thoughtful. 'Maybe I did see something,' he said.

'Something you didn't tell us before?'

'Yeah,' Leach said. 'Something I didn't tell you.'

'Why didn't you tell us?' Gently asked.

'Reasons,' Leach said. 'I had my reasons. Maybe I could see it looked bad for Elton. I don't like sicking the screws on a customer.'

'Even though he might be a murderer?' Gently asked.

'Elton ain't no murderer,' Leach said. 'But that was the way the screws were looking at it, that he'd got a grudge and knocked Lister off.'

'What was it you didn't tell us?' Gently asked.

'Well,' Leach said, 'I broke up a row they was having.'

He licked his lips, flashed a probing look at Gently. Gently wasn't looking at Leach at all. He'd just noticed that the round mirror which hung on the half-landing of the stairs reflected another, higher, mirror, which gave a view down the bar. It was neat. He could see the blonde paying change into the till.

'Here in the milk bar?' he said.

'Yeah,' Leach said. 'That's right.'

'Nobody else mentioned it,' Gently said.

'Well,' Leach said, 'it was in the toilet.'

'Tell me what happened,' Gently said.

'Yeah, in the toilet,' Leach said. 'About ten o'clock, I think it was, the band was having its refreshments. So I went into the toilet and there were these charlies shouting the odds. Elton was going to knock Lister's block off, he'd swiped his girlfriend or some caper. I could see he meant it too, he'd got an ugly look in his eye. So I broke it up. I give them the warning. Round about ten o'clock, that was.'

'Nice of you to remember,' Gently said.

'Yeah,' Leach said. He put the lid on the box.

'We might never have known about it,' Gently said.

Leach tied on the ribbon, placed the box on the pile.

Another customer had come into the bar upstairs, a dingy old man with the appearance of a pensioner. He seemed to be having quite a conversation with the blonde whose doubtfulness was expressed by her attitude and gestures. Leach looked at the mirrors, then at Gently. He patted the box, rearranged the ribbon.

'That's just a dodge of mine,' he said. 'Got to keep an eye on the till when you're down here.'

'On your customers, too,' Gently said.

'Well,' Leach said, 'they don't all come from Mayfair.'

Now the old man had produced an envelope and handed it to the blonde. The blonde turned her back to open it, then nodded, glancing at the cellar entrance. She reached underneath the bar.

'Now see this mike—' Leach began, moving.

'Hold it.' Gently pushed him aside.

What the blonde had handed over was a box of chocolates.

Gently was up on the instant, ran down the cellar and up the stairs. Leach came bolting after him shouting, trying to catch hold of his jacket. The old man was opening the door to go out. He stopped in surprise as the two men rushed in. Gently grabbed the box away from him, planted himself panting against the door. The blonde chose the moment to let go a scream. A customer knocked over a chair as he jumped to his feet.

'You give that back to him!' Leach was shouting. 'You give that back to him, or I'll do you!'

'Get over there,' Gently ordered him. 'He'll have the box after I've seen it.'

'What's going on?' said the customer, a navvy.

'Police,' Gently said. 'In pursuit of a felony.'

'It's a bloody lie!' Leach shouted, white-faced. 'It's him committed felony – he's pinched those chocolates!'

'They're not mine,' the old man was quavering. 'Please give them back to me, they belong to someone else.'

Gently motioned to the navvy. 'Guard this door,' he said. The navvy looked stupid, but he moved in front of the door. Gently took the box to a table, stripped the ribbon from it and lifted the lid. Under brown corrugated wrapping lay a neat layer of chocolates.

'Look at them,' Leach was beginning. 'Bleeding chocolates, that's all.'

But Gently had scooped the chocolates out and lifted the separator that was under them. He stood back.

'Just chocolates?'

The second layer was of cigarettes. Slightly brownish, loosely made, there would be four to five hundred of them.

'Gawd,' Leach said, 'gawd.' His face was a greyish mess.

'Any comment?' Gently asked.

'Yeah,' Leach said. 'I didn't know about them.'

'Save it,' Gently said. He turned to the old man, who stood pop-eyed. 'What do you know about it?' he asked. 'Where did you get the money for these?'

The old man swallowed, shook his head. 'I was asked to come in and get them,' he said. 'A young man gave me ten shillings to collect them. He said there was someone here who he didn't want to see.'

'Where were you taking them?' Gently rapped.

The old man winced. 'Just over in the car park. I was out for my airing when this young man accosted me. He's waiting there by his motorcycle for me to bring them back.'

Gently hesitated, picked up the box. 'Take me to him,' he said. He looked at the navvy. 'See these people don't leave,' he ordered him. 'They're to stay right where they are, not to move from this room. If they try, put your head out and bawl for the police and assistance.'

He pushed the pensioner through the door, took his

arm across the street. The park by now was pretty solid with cars and several people were moving amongst them.

'How was he dressed?' Gently muttered.

'He was dressed for motorcycling,' said the pensioner. 'If we keep this side of the cars he shouldn't see us till we're nearly up to him.'

They kept to that side of the cars, the pensioner trotting along jerkily. When they were three-quarters of the way across he pulled hard on Gently's arm.

'He's over there,' he whispered, 'by that fire-hydrant place.'

'Keep with me,' Gently said. He disengaged his arm.

But just then a motor roared on the other side of the hydrant station. Gently belted through the cars, hurled himself round the small building. He caught only a glimpse of a powerful bike cornering sharply into a back street, its black-leathered rider lying it close, its registration plate invisible. The pensioner came stuttering after Gently.

'That's him!' he exclaimed, 'That's him!'

Gently stood clutching his box. 'Yes,' he said. 'That's him.'

He returned to the milk bar where the navvy remained dutifully guarding the entrance. Leach was sitting on one of the bar-stools, the blonde was snivelling into a handkerchief. Leach's eyes glittered when he saw Gently come back with the pensioner only, but he didn't say anything, kept his face sullenly averted. Gently confronted him.

'Who was he?' he asked.

'How should I know?' Leach said. 'I don't know nothing about this caper. I'm being used, that's what it is.'

'You,' Gently said to the blonde. 'Who were you expecting to pick that box up?'

'She don't know nothing,' Leach put in quickly. 'She wouldn't be such a bloody fool as to know anything.'

'That's right,' the blonde sobbed, 'I don't know nothing. I serve behind the bar, that's all I do.'

'Give me that envelope,' Gently said.

'I don't know what you mean,' sobbed the blonde.

'Just the envelope,' Gently said. 'The one this gentleman here handed you.'

'He didn't hand me no envelope.'

'Let's keep polite about it,' Gently said. 'He handed you a fat manilla envelope, after which you gave him the chocolates.'

'It's down the front of her dress,' said the navvy unexpectedly. 'I saw her shove it there while you were out.'

'So?' Gently said.

The blonde looked murderous. She felt in her bosom, tossed the envelope on the bar. Gently lifted it by one corner and let the contents slip out. They were a bundle of forty or so pound notes, old ones, held together with a rubber band.

'That's a lot of money for a box of chocolates.'

'It was owed us,' Leach snapped. 'We don't know nothing about what was in the chocolates.'

'But you'll know who owed you the money.'

Leach made a rude suggestion. 'Bloody find out,' he added. 'We've said all we're going to say.'

Gently sat amiably on another bar-stool. He slowly filled and lit his pipe. When it was alight he blew two rings, placing one of them in the other.

'You're in a bit of a jam, Leach,' he said.

Leach was impolite again.

'You'll be going away,' Gently continued. 'You'll be going away for quite a spell. This isn't the only box, is it? You've been filling some more down in the cellar. You've got a stock of reefers here, you're the local distributor for the top boys.'

'I'm being used, I tell you,' Leach said. 'I've never seen them things before.'

Gently shook his head. 'You won't make it stand up, Joe. Look at it squarely. You're due for a rest.'

'I ought to have pitched you,' Leach said, spitting.

'We'll let that pass,' Gently said. 'But you're in a jam right up to your ears, and if you're wise you'll stop trying to buck it. Because a kind word could make a difference to you, Joe. And I'm the one who could put in the kind word.'

'You think I can't see it coming?' Leach said.

'Who was this box for?' Gently asked.

'I wouldn't know, would I?' Leach said, sneering. It don't happen to have a name and address.'

'Where are you getting the stuff from, Joe?'

'Look for the trademark on it,' said Leach.

'It'll be maybe worth a year to you, Joe.'

'Yeah, but I value my health higher,' Leach said.

'I'll tell you something else,' the navvy said. 'I keep my eyes about me, I do.'

'You keep quiet, you bastard,' Leach snapped.

'You better look in that coffee machine,' the navvy said.

Leach came off the stool in a whirlwind of fists. Gently caught him, heaved, sent him crashing among the tables. He went to the coffee machine, the lid of which was awry. He looked inside. In the bubbling black coffee floated a green-covered notebook. He fished it out with a fork.

'Blimey!' said the navvy, looking at Leach.

'Nice work,' Gently said. 'We could use your sort in the Force.'

He separated some pages of the sodden notebook. It contained dates, figures, and some notes of money. And on the inside of the cover appeared a telephone number with a London code prefixed to it.

'Well, well,' he said. 'You've been a little careless, Joe.'

Leach kept sitting on the floor. He said a number of things that were not nice.

CHAPTER SIX

GENTLY HUNG ON at Castlebridge while the local police were in action, but neither Leach nor the blonde seemed inclined to be more helpful. Two other counter assistants arrived at the milk bar during the morning, but on interrogation it was soon apparent that they knew nothing of the trade in reefers. A considerable haul was made in the cellar. Leach had concealed his store under the planking of the dais. It consisted of fifteen sauce-bottle cartons each containing a thousand reefers, while another three thousand were found packed in the boxes of chocolates.

The local inspector, Cartwright, was dubiously cordial towards Gently, at times was plainly miffed by this discovery in his area. When he elicited that Gently had wasted no time in talking to the Yard about the matter he became respectfully frigid and held himself at a distance.

Gently's call had been to Pagram, his opposite number in the Central Office, giving him the telephone number he had found in Leach's notebook.

'Is this helping your case?' Pagram had asked him.

Gently didn't know himself. 'If it takes you Bethnal way,' he'd said, 'I shall like to know about that. A lot of the overspill population has come to Latchford from Bethnal. You know we've got Sid Bixley here. Keep his name where you can see it.'

Pagram'd chuckled. 'Is he your bunnie?'

'I'm interested,' Gently had said. 'He's got an alibi that seems to cover him, but it's only sixty per cent proof.'

The trouble was there was no way of bringing Bixley's alibi to proof. That he'd left the milk bar fifteen minutes after Lister had been established by fairly reliable witnesses. Some Castlebridge acquaintances who knew them both had seen Lister leaving early, they'd invited him to have one for the road and had been surprised by his abrupt refusal. Then fifteen minutes had elapsed while they drank that last shake, and when they left they had been accompanied by Bixley and Anne Wicks. In between Elton had left. He'd been seen leaving soon after Lister. Yet it was possible that this order had been changed over the twenty or so miles to the scene of the crash. Lister might have ridden the first part slowly, Elton might have lost some time, say, at Oldmarket. The alibi was a good one but it didn't completely exclude Bixley.

In a quiet corner of the milk bar Gently had interrogated the pensioner. His name was Edwin Jukes. He badly wanted to be helpful. He recounted carefully how he'd met the 'young man' as he was skirting along the car park, and how he'd been saluted as 'Dad' and offered the ten shillings to fetch the chocolates.

'How old would this young man be?' Gently asked.

'That I couldn't say,' Jukes quavered.

'Twenty? Thirty?' Gently suggested.

'Oh, he was a youngster all right,' Jukes said.

'What colour were his hair and eyes?' asked Gently.

'Well,' Jukes said, 'he was wearing a hat thing. I didn't notice his eyes. I don't see very grand. I'm nigh on eighty if I live to see Christmas.'

'Was he tall?' Gently asked.

'He was taller than I am,' Jukes said. 'And I'm five foot seven, if that's any help.'

'Did he speak like a local boy?'

Jukes was baffled by that one. 'I can't,' he said, 'say he did, nor I can't say he didn't.'

He was able however to confirm Gently's impression that the youth was dressed all in black: black helmet, black leathers, black boots, and black gloves. He'd produced the envelope from a breast pocket without removing the gloves and had promised to pay the ten shillings when Jukes returned with the chocolates. The person he wished to avoid, he said, was the blonde at the counter.

'There's nothing else at all you can tell me about him?' Gently asked.

'Why yes,' said Jukes. 'He was a very familiar young man.'

'You mean you've seen him before?' Gently asked.

'Oh, no, no,' Jukes said. 'But he called me Dad, and I'm not partial to that.'

Gently had lunch at the Copper Kettle, then called back at the Castlebridge H.Q., but the prints on the envelope, which he'd asked to have processed, were only those of Jukes and the blonde. Inspector Cartwright was obsequious.

'I'm sorry we can't be more helpful,' he said. 'Perhaps you'll have better luck with the Yard.'

'Yeah,' Gently said. 'And thanks.'

After lunch it had turned cloudy. He was stuck with traffic as far as Oldmarket. An R.A.F. trailer carrying a bomber fuselage was holding his line of traffic in check. At the top of Oldmarket High it turned right and brought everything to a standstill, spreading itself in little jerks till it was clear across both lanes. Past Oldmarket things improved and he was able to cruise in the sixes. People were still at lunch, maybe, they weren't yet cluttering up the roads. He was beyond Barford Mills and watching for a sight of the Gallows Tree when he first noticed in his mirror the two motorcycles behind him.

Side by side they were riding, around a quarter of a mile behind him, linked together so closely that for a moment he took them for a small car. He watched them corner. It was a precision movement, the two bikes leaning over in concert. And even at the distance of a quarter of a mile he could see that the riders were clad in black.

He gave the 75 some gas, let her press up into the eights. For a while he lost his twin pursuers behind a truck and a double bend. Then he saw them again, closing in slightly, cutting the distance by a hundred yards. They settled down at that distance. They were obviously stalking him.

Gently shrugged, kept the 75 skimming along at eight and a half. They could chase him if they wanted to, but there was no percentage in that. It would take more than motorcyclists to stop him, if they had any such intention, and on a frequented main road it would be foolish to attempt it in any case. All the same he was very curious about those two black-leathered riders. He found himself wishing he was in a squad car with radio contact with the local patrols.

The Gallows Tree rose on his left and he crested the ridge into Five Mile Drove. The road lay dully stretching ahead under the grey cloak of October wrack. There was little on it. He pressed the 75 harder. She began to labour at the top of her compass. With the slope assisting she drifted into the nines and held it there, several short of the century. He glanced in his mirror. They were still coming. More, they were closing the distance again. They were bettering his speed by a sizable margin, ten, maybe fifteen miles an hour. And this time they weren't settling behind him: they were coming up to pass.

He eased the 75 slightly to give himself a margin of acceleration, watched them leaping now towards him, their handlebars pretty well touching. They wore goggles and black scarves which covered the bottom halves of their faces, their bikes appeared to be sheeted in some way: he could see the black plastic flapping. And still they came, straight behind him, making no move to pull out. It was as though they intended to ride flush into the rear of the 75.

He took his eyes off the mirror – very well, it was their funeral! – and kept the 75 very straight down the empty stretch ahead. He refused to look at the mirror. He knew instinctively when they were up with him. He was checking his breath, waiting for the crash, certain that a crash was going to occur. Then he heard a roar above the boom of his engine. The two bikes appeared. They'd come up one on each side of him. For a couple of seconds the inside bike was bucking the bald, worn, verge: then they were through, closing up, streaking away glove by glove. He stared intently at the diminishing machines, but their plates were shrouded in the drumming black plastic.

He found himself biting hard on his pipe. It was a pretty manœuvre, that one! If he'd chanced to swerve a couple of inches there'd have been a fresh body in Five Mile Drove. He dropped his speed down to the sixes, let them go right away from him, saw them dwindle into dots in the misty aisle of the Chase. But the dots did not quite dwindle. Instead, they separated in drunken curves. For a moment he was at a loss to interpret what it was they were doing. Then he realized: they had turned. They were coming back for another attempt.

It was too crazy for anything. He guessed directly what was intended. He glanced quickly at his mirror, then moved out towards the crown of the road. He would have to cooperate, there was no alternative. To try to avoid them would bring disaster. He had to play along, as crazy as they were, and pray to high heaven they could bring it off. He held the 75 poised, kept her steady at six and a half. He said his prayer to high heaven and braced himself for what was coming.

This time their combined speeds must have been well over a hundred and fifty. The two machines hurtled towards him like missiles fired from a gun. He fought the instinct to close his eyes, to jam at the brakes, to swerve away. For a moment it seemed to him physically impossible to go on driving straight at them. Then the moment passed and he felt an icy detachment. The break came, they flicked apart, scythed howling by his two wings. A spark of elation glowed in him. He hadn't diverged by a hairsbreadth. Only, he noticed with some surprise, his foot was hard down on the accelerator.

They turned and caught him again before the end of the Drove, but the slow overtake from behind now seemed comparatively tame. They were weaving slightly after they passed him, a victory roll it might have been. He pulled the stops out, trying to hold them, but they surged effortlessly away from the 75. Was there any chance of intercepting them? He made a mental check of the road ahead. It passed no phone box, no houses, up to the outskirts of Latchford. All they needed in the meantime were a few seconds to strip off that sheeting. After that they were unidentifiable, merely another pair of motorcyclists . . .

He eased down to a more reasonable speed and drew resignedly at his cold pipe. They'd got away with it for the moment, there was no point in flogging along on their tails. Better to start thinking out what was the significance of that incident, which he was sure had been planned with a deal of thoroughness and knowledge. He drove thoughtfully back into Latchford. He passed the Sun and kept going. He turned right into the Norwich Road, parked at the First and Last café.

Outside the First and Last café were standing six motorcycles and each motorcycle of the six had black plastic sheeting laced over it. The sheeting was cut so that it covered the tank and made a triangle with the pillion and back axle, thus concealing, except to an expert, the brand make of the machine.

Gently got out and walked over to them. It was very quiet inside the café. He walked along the row of motorcycles, stooping to place a hand near each engine. They were cool though not cold. They hadn't been run for some time. The plastic sheetings had no mud on them. The number plates were stark and legal. He dusted his hand, nodded his head, walked into the café.

The six owners of the bikes sat at a table near the door, in front of each a milkshake and a sandwich on a plate. They were all dressed in black leathers and wore silk scarves round their necks. Their black gauntlets and black helmets were placed by the side of their plates. They sat silently and without moving. Only their eyes turned to Gently. In the background, his cheek twitching, Tony was doing something with a teapot.

'Tony,' Gently said, 'I'll have a milkshake and a sandwich.'

Tony dropped the teapot noisily, grabbed a shaker and slopped milk into it.

'Whata would you like?' he gabbled.

'Same as the chaps,' Gently said.

'They got banana,' Tony said.

'Make mine banana,' said Gently.

He took a leisurely survey of the premises. Two transport men were also sitting there. They looked bored. They weren't eating and they didn't catch Gently's eye. At the silent table was a seventh chair and a vacant space on the table in front of it. Gently paid for his order, took it to the space, placed his trilby by it, and sat on the chair.

'Now,' he said, 'as a matter of form, we'll take the names and addresses first.'

He looked encouragingly round the table. No one answered him a word.

'You,' he said to a squash-nosed boy, 'your name is Salmon, so I'm told.'

'Like what's it to you?' Salmon said. 'We haven't been doing nothing, screw.'

'We'll come to that,' Gently said. 'You live in Barnham Road, don't you?'

'Tell him, Jack,' said a thick-featured youngster. 'We go for this screw knowing who we are.'

They gave him their names and addresses. Gently wrote them in his notebook. They were Jack Salmon, Jeff Cook, Pete Starling, Bill Hallman, Frankie Knights, and Tommy Grimstead, Hallman being the thick-featured one. Tony watched this going on with increasing agitation. The transport men seemed restive. One of them was heeling the leg of his chair.

'Right,' Gently said. 'Now just for the book, how long have you been here?'

'Like an hour and a half,' Hallman said. 'Ask anyone how long we've been here.'

'Tony?' Gently said.

'It's the truth what they say,' Tony said. 'They been here the hour and a half, mister. I don't wanta no trouble around here.'

'You won't get it,' Gently said. 'Not if you keep your nose clean. What do these other two gentlemen say?'

The transport men were looking sheepish.

'That's about right,' one of them muttered. 'We've been here an hour, and they were here in front of us.'

'You want to get away?' Gently asked.

''Bout time we were going,' the man said.

'I should get away,' Gently said. 'You've nothing left to stop for now.'

The two men got to their feet hastily. One of them stumbled as he went through the door. Tony was clutching his arms anguishedly as though they were bothering him with cramp.

'Good,' Gently said, 'that's the inessentials. Now we can get down to business perhaps. What are the six of you sitting in here for – why aren't you at work like other people?'

'Like we work when we want to,' Hallman said. 'Is there a law against it, screw?'

'Yuh,' Salmon said, 'what gives with you, screw? We can sit in here as long as we like.'

'So you weren't told off for it?' Gently said.

'We weren't told nothing,' Hallman said.

'You weren't told to tie those sheets on your bikes.'

'Not nothing we was told about,' Hallman said.

'Then you just tied them on, did you?' Gently said. 'You just got the same idea. All six of you.'

'Yuh, that's about it,' Hallman said. 'Like we just got the same idea about that.'

'And about meeting in here?'

'Yuh,' Hallman said.

'And bribing a couple of transport drivers to witness your alibi for you.'

Hallman stirred, his eyes rolled a little as he tried to keep them fixed on Gently's. 'Like whose saying we bribed them, you tell me screw,' he said.

'It's true anyway,' Salmon put in. 'We dug you feeling round our engines. We've been sitting here since after lunch, and you know it, screw.'

'So they were only paid to tell the truth,' Gently said.

'Yuh,' Salmon said. 'That's why we paid them. Like you'd come in here trying to hang us up somehow, and wouldn't go much on what Tony told you.'

'And why should I come in here doing that?'

'Screws,' Salmon said, 'we know them.'

'You knew I was going to come in here?'

'Yuh,' Salmon said. 'No.'

'Which way do you want it?' Gently asked.

'Like it's none of your business,' Salmon said. 'We can sit here if we want to. And we can pay money if we want to.'

'For an alibi for nothing?'

'Like never mind!' Hallman said.

'I don't mind,' Gently said. 'I'm just interested, that's all.'

He sucked some of the milkshake through his straws and took a bite from the sandwich. None of the others was eating or drinking. They sat still. They looked unhappy. When some traffic went by they would all glance out of the window. Tony was also watching the traffic, he was leaning nervously on his elbows.

'How much longer,' Gently asked, 'do you think I ought to wait here?'

They looked startled. Hallman glared, Salmon pouted and dropped his eyes.

'I've other business,' Gently said. 'But I don't want to spoil the fun. You've taken some pains to lay it on, and I wouldn't like to disappoint you.'

'Smart,' Hallman said. 'You're being smart, screw, aren't you?'

'That's a screw's business,' Gently said.

'Yuh,' Hallman said. 'A screw's business.'

'You can sling your hook,' Salmon said. 'We don't care what you do.'

'Tony,' Gently said, 'what do you say?'

'I don't wanta the trouble,' Tony moaned.

'Shut your trap, Tony,' Hallman said. 'Who says there's going to be trouble?'

Tony wrung his arms again, tried to wind himself into the counter. Time crept by. Gently finished his sandwich, got only a bubbling from the bottom of his glass. The general unhappiness was increasing, nobody was looking at Gently now. Salmon was frowning in a ferocious way. The faces of some of the others were flushed. Only Gently, lighting his pipe, looked relaxed and mildly amused.

'Set up a couple more shakes, Tony.'

Tony came out of the counter with a jerk.

'You want I maka you two more shakes?'

'Yes,' Gently said. 'Then we'll have them ready.'

'Smart,' Hallman said bitterly.

'Just not dumb,' Gently said.

'You don't know nothing,' Hallman said. 'Big-headed screws being smart.'

Tony made the shakes. The timing was good. He was pouring out the second one when the two motorcycles pulled in. Nobody looked out of the window, Gently was sitting with his back to it. They heard the engines being killed, the rests kicked down, footsteps. The footsteps stopped in the doorway. Gently jetted out some smoke.

'Come in,' he said. 'Don't be shy. You've kept us waiting twenty minutes.'

'Well, look who's here,' Bixley said, strutting in and making a posture. 'Like our big-deal screw from the Smoke has come slumming again.' He stood feet apart, arms on hips, staring mockingly at Gently. He was wearing a windcheater and jeans. A nervous, dark-eyed youngster accompanied him.

'Yeah, slumming,' Bixley grinned. 'That's the tag for what he's doing. Waiting for you and me, Alfie, thinking up some jazz to put across us. Isn't that nice of the screw, Alfie? Don't he look a real square's square? Slumming here along with some jees and thinking up jazz to put across us!'

'Have I met you?' Gently said to Alfie.

'Meet the screw, Alfie,' said Bixley. 'Man, he's got big eyes for you. Like keep it down or you'll get slapped.'

'What's your surname?' Gently asked.

'Tell the screw,' Bixley said.

'Alfie Curtis,' Alfie said. He looked worried, kept his eyes down.

'Now he'll ask you questions,' Bixley said. 'That's what screws do, they ask questions, Alfie. Like where you've been since lunch, that sort of crap. You know?'

'I know,' Alfie said. It didn't seem to make him happier.

'You'll love this screw,' Bixley said. 'He's a real wild screw, man.'

He swung round on his heel, strode across to the counter. Tony pointed a trembling finger at the two milkshakes. Bixley pulled off his gloves and grabbed a shake off the counter. He jerked the straws on to the floor, swallowed down the shake at one draught. He burped. He wiped his mouth with the back of his hand.

'So ask your questions, screw,' he said. 'Something hanging you up, is there?'

Gently smiled, shook his head. 'I know the answers,' he said. 'Screws don't ask questions when they know the answers.'

'He's being smart,' Hallman said. 'He makes you sick, he's so smart, Sid.'

'Like that, is it?' Bixley said. 'He comes out here to be smart, does he?'

'Yuh, smart,' Hallman said.

'He comes to the right place,' Bixley said. 'We've got a way with smart screws. They get to wondering how smart they are.'

He came back stiff-legged to the table, stood right beside Gently.

'Let's hear those answers, screw,' he said. 'Could be they don't quite fit the questions.'

'Are you worried about it?' Gently asked.

'Like do as I say,' Bixley said. 'You're a long way from the screw-shop, and nobody's going to ring it for you.'

'You'd better sit down,' Gently said.

'Like there isn't a chair,' Bixley said.

'You can pull one up from the next table.'

'Like there isn't room,' Bixley said.

Gently shrugged. 'Well, what do you want to know?'

'Just the answers,' Bixley said. 'Like where you think Alfie's been since lunchtime, and where I've been. That's all, screw.'

Gently puffed. 'Alfie's been out riding with you,' he said. 'You picked him up after lunch, said it was a nice day for a ride. Then you rode off towards Norwich or made a detour in that direction. And now you've just come back and you've dropped in here for a milkshake.'

'Crazy, isn't he?' Bixley said. 'I wonder how he knew all that?'

'Have I got it right?' Gently asked.

'Yeah,' Bixley said. 'Somebody told you.'

'Here's some more,' Gently said. 'Alfie was thrilled to have you ask him. He hasn't had a bike for long. He doesn't ride as well as you, Sid.'

'Didn't I say he was wild?' Bixley inquired. 'This is the wildest screw ever. How long have you had that bike, Alfie?'

'Like two and a half months,' Alfie said.

'And how do you ride it?' Bixley asked.

'I get along,' Alfie said.

'But not like me?' Bixley said.

'Not like you,' Alfie admitted. 'You're the mostest on a bike, Sid. Don't reckon I'll ever ride like you.'

Bixley stooped, advanced his face towards Gently's. 'You notice how right you're being, screw?' he said. 'You've got the answers, so like you'd better stay with them. Then you'll really be smart. For a screw.'

'I hadn't finished,' Gently said.

'Don't come it clever, screw,' said Bixley.

'There's this morning, too,' Gently said. 'I could guess a little bit about that.'

'I'm warning you, screw,' Bixley said.

Gently puffed over his head. 'You were out riding this morning, Sid,' he said. 'You've done a lot of riding today.'

Bixley came right close to him. 'Keep going, screw,' he said. 'But just remember how handsome you look when you're healthy. Remember that.'

'I'll remember,' Gently said, 'and thanks for the compliment, Sid. You went out riding the heath roads this morning and I doubt whether you met a single soul.'

Bixley relaxed. 'You're the most,' he said.

'Right again?' Gently asked.

'You should be on TV, screw,' Bixley said. 'The way you know answers is real comic.'

'I've heard so many,' Gently said. 'The trouble is they're not true. Now Elton's story sounded true. I wonder why there's such a difference?'

He was on his feet and the chair kicked away from him before Bixley's fist began to travel: the fist missed by six inches and Bixley was clubbed down with a right.

Hallman swung a blow that connected but then somehow he dived into the floor. The others were struggling up from the table when the table heaved forward and sent them in a tangle. Alfie decided to keep out of things. Tony had vanished behind his counter.

'Get that bastard!' Bixley was shouting, spitting blood from a cut mouth. 'Don't let him get away. We're going to do the bleeder now!'

He wobbled furiously to his feet, but he was obviously shaken by the blow he'd got. The others didn't seem keen to second him. They were sorting themselves out from the furniture discretely. Gently stood calmly, back to the wall. His pipe was still between his teeth.

'You think too slowly, Sid,' he said.

'You bastard, I'll get you for this!' Bixley spat.

'Perhaps you're short of chocolates,' Gently said.

Bixley swore, but with little conviction.

Tony rose tremblingly from behind the counter. 'P-please,' he stuttered, 'p-pleasa, p-pleasa!'

'You're all right, Tony,' Gently said. 'Give Sid some water to wash his mouth out.'

'Like what's going on here?' inquired a voice from the door. Deeming stood there. He looked immense in his crash helmet.

'Hullo, Dicky,' Gently said. 'I had to quieten them before you got here.'

CHAPTER SEVEN

DEEMING WASN'T LOOKING pleased. His eyes went frostily to Bixley. There was a sudden silence in the café. Nobody seemed inclined to break it. Jack Salmon was still on the floor and he remained where he was. Jeff Cook was picking up a chair. He let the chair stop in his hand. The rest went similarly still. Only Tony was hugging and wringing himself. The sound of a passing car came precisely. One could also hear Bixley's heavy breathing.

'I thought,' Deeming said tightly, 'I told you to keep it down with the screws. Like flipping the lid was square action. Like jeebies ought to be above it.'

Nobody said anything. Bixley dribbled a spittle of blood on the floor. Deeming came slowly out of the doorway, took a stand before Bixley.

'So what's it about, Sid?' he said. 'You seem to have been in amongst it. How come you got that poke in the mouth and like there's been a landslide in the neighbourhood?'

'He was needling me again,' Bixley jerked. 'Like I can't stand that screw needling me.'

'Yuh, he was needling him,' Hallman said. 'That's how it was, ain't it, blokes?'

'Yuh, he was needling him,' several of them repeated. 'That's how it was. He was needling Sid.'

'So then all you cool cats flip your lids?'

'Like I couldn't help it,' Bixley said. 'He jabbed me rotten. He was being smart. Like he was trying to make me poke him.'

'And like he succeeded,' said Deeming scathingly, 'if the blood you're spitting is anything to go by. I thought I could depend on you, Sid. I thought I'd talked some cool sense into you.'

'Yuh, but there's a limit,' Bixley said.

'A limit like yours,' said Deeming, 'is dangerous.'

'I tell you I wasn't going to poke him,' Bixley said. 'Just lean on him some. I was trying to lean on him.'

'And like he leaned back.'

'Yuh,' Bixley snarled. 'Like he did. And I took a poke.'

'Did you think he was a pushover?' Deeming said. 'Did you think you could lean on him and he wouldn't lean back?' He swung round from Bixley, turned to Gently. 'So what's the score, screw?' he said. 'Are you hanging Sid up on the grounds he's taken a poke at you?'

Gently shook his head slowly. 'It wouldn't be worth it, would it?' he said.

'You dig him?' Bixley snapped out. 'It's all needle, needle, needle.'

'Like,' Deeming said sharply, 'you'll let me handle this, Sid. This screw isn't so square as a lot of screws you'll meet.'

'Thank you, Dicky,' Gently said.

'I could pan him,' Bixley said.

'But what you will do,' Deeming said, 'is to pick up Tony's chairs and table.'

There was a scramble to pick them up. Bixley didn't join in it. He grabbed a chair, flopped on it heavily, sat licking at his lip and eyeing Gently. Deeming singled out Hallman to collect the broken plates and glasses. He gave the pile a casual scrutiny, laid a pound note on the counter.

'Will this cover it, Tony?' he asked.

Tony nodded, screwing his face up.

'Sorry,' Deeming said, 'about the dust-up. It won't happen again, Tony. You've got my word for it.'

'I don't lika the trouble, Mister Deeming,' Tony said.

'Me neither,' said Deeming. 'It's screwball. And like I've talked to these guys some more I'll put some hip into them yet. I'm not a jee for trouble, Tony.'

'No, Mister Deeming,' Tony said.

'That's not the way to be real,' Deeming said. 'That's just the square action coming out.'

He came back to Gently.

'I saw your car,' he said. 'Like I was just going out for a spin. I wondered if you'd care to ride along.'

'With you, pillion?' Gently asked.

'Sure, pillion,' Deeming said. 'Have you ridden a Bonneville before? Man, they're cool, they're refrigerative.'

Gently hesitated. All of them were watching him. He dropped a couple of reflective puffs.

'I've come along this far,' he said. 'I might as well go the whole distance.'

'Crazy, you'll go for it,' Deeming said. 'Jack, lend the screw your helmet and goggles. Man, I can guarantee this will send you. I dig your style. This'll put you way out.'

His slate eyes glinted a smile at Gently. Bixley spat some more blood on the floor.

They rode back into town, down the High Street, past the Sun. The cloud had thinned now to a light haze and the light was golden and the air warm. Gently's helmet was rather small for him, felt like a crown perched on his head. He felt a little ridiculous straddling the pillion and holding Deeming by his waist. The slipstream plucked at his light trousers though they were tucked into his socks. Where only the socks protected his ankles were two bands of chilled flesh. He had a sensation of insecurity. His seat on the bike seemed precarious. He was naked and unfenced from the streets and buildings that flickered by him.

Beyond the Sun they crossed the bridge and headed, as he knew they would, in the direction of Castlebridge. On the short run through the town Deeming had shown himself a talented rider. He rode steadily, at an even pace, seeming to adjust the traffic to suit himself. Now, as they passed the delimit, he twisted the throttle open with a smooth precision. The machine seemed to be soaring away from Gently, as though it were climbing and he was sliding off. He clung tighter, crouched over Deeming. The slipstream punched him like icy dough. The road, a streaky grey death, unreamed a few inches below his feet. The note of the engine was a pummelling throb and the heat from it was roasting the insides of his shins. Traffic exploded on their right. Sometimes it howled past Gently's elbow. A monstrous truck rose up ahead, slanted to the left, went by in madness. They were into the trees in under two minutes. The trees were ghosts. They didn't seem to belong.

Deeming's back pushed hard at Gently and the road came wheeling up from the right.

'Roll!' Deeming bawled over his shoulder. 'Christ, roll with me, or you'll have us off!'

The road sank back. They were on a straight again. The machine was soaring in its climb to speed. They knifed through traffic that notched both sides of them, the trees sprang open in an insane geometry. Gently had stopped now trying to resist, to brace himself for the violence of disaster. A half-real mirage was all that contained them. It kept falling away from their inevitable onset. Nothing was real except the machine and the two of them. They were out of the world. They were alone, unreachable.

'Roll!' Deeming bawled, pressing backwards.

This time Gently relaxed, leaning with him. The grass verge reeled in a crescendo at their shoulders, stayed with them, slid away into its streaming level.

'You've got it!' Deeming roared. 'Just let yourself go with me. And man, hang on tight. This is where we hit the ton.'

They had come to Five Mile Drove. Its vacuum of straightness was sucking them into it. Like the glorious path of an arrow it split upwards towards the sky. And on the path of that arrow they hung poised in an immaculate balance, the world falling away from them, faded away in divine speed. He felt a curious sense of freedom, a calm almost. He seemed released into a peacefulness, a huge detachment from the diminished physical. In a sort of wonderment he noticed the tree expanding like some black, spiritual flower, at first slowly, then urgently, then rushing into the sky. At the same moment an invisible hand crushed him back from the peace he experienced. The vision, the sensation, was dragged away from him. He was painfully returned to the dull moment.

Deeming slid over on to the level ground that surrounded the tree, bucked joltingly up to it, dropped his feet, cut the engine. Gently's ears were still buzzing, the air felt suddenly hot and thin. His legs were aching. He was aware of pain from the chilled bands around his ankles. Deeming raised his goggles, twisted his head round. His eyes rested on Gently smilingly.

'You get it now, screw,' he asked, 'like the way it was with Lister?'

Gently raised his goggles also. His face was burning and stiff.

'The ton and nineteen,' Deeming said. 'That was cooling it some, screw. That was touching it good and hard. That was way out, way out. And you were getting the kick, screw. Like that's a kick you can't miss. You were on the borders, you know? You were on the borders way out.'

'You're a good rider,' Gently said.

'Yeah,' Deeming said. 'Sid taught me.'

'He's another good rider,' Gently said.

'Sure,' Deeming said. 'That makes two of us.'

'Two good riders,' Gently said.

Deeming gave him a broad grin. 'I like you, screw,' he said. 'You're subtle. You're cool, too, in your Squaresville way.'

He raised his hand, made a gesture of fiddling.

'Like that was just the allegro movement,' he said. 'But that's not all. I've got an adagio for you. Like you're through with the interval I'll make with the baton.'

He pulled his goggles back down, lifted the bike and kicked the starter. They bumped back on the road, pointed towards town again. Deeming rode at a fluent sixty but sixty now seemed a crawl: it took them all of five minutes to put the tree back on the horizon. They approached the scene of Lister's crash, neared the lane that cut in just before it. Deeming slowed and took the lane. Its surface was soft and littered with pine needles. The boughs of the pine trees met above it and the air was moist and resin-scented. The lane went straight for some distance, then slanted left, and again right. They passed an enamelled fire-warning notice with beneath it a stock of beating brooms.

'Like Canada,' Deeming jerked over his shoulder. 'I've seen it like this in Canada, screw.'

There was a deadness and hush among the close-packed trees that seemed to absorb the low throb of the engine.

It continued for above a mile, changing direction in straight slants, rising and falling over shallow ridges, and with occasional surfaces of loose gravel. Then the tall trees knifed away and gave place to a grove of saplings, then the saplings stopped abruptly to reveal a nursery of bush trees. The nursery was fenced with small-mesh netting. It bore the fire-warning plates. The young trees had a bluish bloom and the wistful appearance of bold callowness. Deeming slowed right down through the nursery as though he wanted Gently to take it in. At the end it was protected by twin lines of birches and beyond the birches they were out on the brecks.

Deeming kept to his slow pace. The lane was a barely visible track. About it the brecks went sweeping and rolling in blackish and tawny valleys and ridges. There was nothing to see but these undulations. They moved from one horizon to the other. Their vegetation was bramble, heath, furze, and russet patches of bracken. They lacked landmark or direction. They had apparently no bird-life. They had a silence as of unbelievable age, or as though they were listening. Even their sky seemed lower and stiller and watching the dark stillness beneath.

'Spooky, isn't it?' Deeming commented out of the corner of his mouth. 'You know, I go for this, screw. Like it reminds me of the outback. You ever been down under, screw?'

'No,' Gently said. 'Not yet.'

'You get it just like this,' Deeming said. 'But like it's hotter and the sky's hollow. I had a spell at a station out a bit from Alice. Big drought country, screw, say it's five hundred from Alice. I was herding on the trail, slept in places like this. Mulga trees. Abos. Spooky as hell, it was.'

'On the borders?' Gently asked.

'Yeah, plumb on them,' Deeming said. 'Like I hadn't thrown that jazz then, but I was getting the kick all the same. And the kick you get here, maybe you get it a bit stronger. Because like your abos are ghosts, screw, though they're still here, they haven't moved out.'

'It's a theory,' Gently said.

'Too right it is,' said Deeming.

They went on riding. At times the track seemed to disappear altogether. Its line was straight, it followed a depression or climbed a ridge indifferently. From the top of the ridges you could see some miles, but all those miles were more breck: there was only the black Chase far behind, perhaps a couple of firs far ahead. The sky was whitish without gradation. The sun was a brightness over to the left.

At last they did arrive at something that made an event in the sameness. It was a level depression of a few acres, grown with scanty, brownish grass. At either side it had hummocky ground and on one of the hummocks were the two firs they had seen. The track passed by the nearer hummocks and crossed the depression to a point near the fir trees. Deeming followed it there and stopped. He killed the engine, thrust up his goggles.

'What do you make of this?' he asked.

Gently climbed stiffly off the bike. He was getting tired of his pillion-riding, tired of the weight of the helmet.

'It could have been camping ground,' he said.

Deeming shook his head. 'No water, cobber. The abos didn't build camps away from water. Like you must give them a little sense.'

'What do you say it is?' Gently asked.

'Well, it could be a holy place,' Deeming said. He had

his eyes fixed hard on Gently. 'You reckon it might be a holy place?' he said.

Gently didn't say anything. He felt for his pipe and filled it. After a moment Deeming propped the bike, fetched out a case, lit a cigarette.

'Like these broken bits here could have been barrows,' he said. 'Maybe some squares bust them up, looking for loot and whatnot.'

'Maybe,' Gently said.

'You think it's likely?' Deeming asked.

'I wouldn't know,' Gently said. 'Better ask an archaeologist.'

'Yeah, but I'm curious,' Deeming said. 'I get a wild kick out here. I stop here long and it sends me, I don't know who or where I am. You ever get a kick like that?'

'I'm too much of a square,' Gently said.

'I was out here this morning,' Deeming said. 'You know? It sent me, I was gone for hours.'

'Which particular hours?' Gently said.

'Like you've beat me there,' said Deeming. 'But man, I touch it here so hard it's a wonder I get back in again.'

'Try eating chocolates,' Gently said.

'Yuh?' Deeming said. 'What's that for a crack?'

Gently shrugged, climbed up the hummock, took some steps round its perimeter. It was very roughly circular and the middle and one side seemed to have been excavated. The hollow was carpeted with needles and fir cones. There lay in it also a cigarette packet and two or three ends. He climbed down the side of the hollow and retrieved them. They were fresh. They hadn't been in the dew.

'You smoke Player's?' he demanded of Deeming.

Deeming grinned. 'Like I do, screw,' he said.

'They'd be Player's,' Gently said, 'in your case?'

Deeming took out his case, snapped it open, showed them.

'I needn't have asked that, need I?' Gently said.

'Sure,' Deeming said. 'You're a screw. It checks. I tell you I've been here all the morning, and like you want to prove it. That's being a screw.'

'Why should I want to know you'd been here all the morning?'

Deeming opened his big palms. 'You tell me,' he said.

'I'll tell you something,' Gently said. 'There's a lot of imagination being used.'

'Imagination?' Deeming said.

'Yes. And Bixley hasn't got much.'

Deeming made a face at him. 'You're being subtle, screw,' he said. 'Man, you're the one for the sly dig. It sends me, the way you give it spin.'

Gently looked at him, puffing. He dropped the packet and ends back in the hollow.

The track bore to the right past the depression, or perhaps was joined by a second track. Neither track was distinct enough to suggest which way it was. But they rode away from the two firs at a right angle to their line of approach, the depression quickly melting back into the anonymity of the brecks. Deeming was humming to himself. It was a theme of Beethoven's. He rode faster on this return leg, but still not very fast. The sun had strengthened as it began to set and was filling the hollows with slaty shadow. Some low mist was forming. It kept in the hollows.

Eventually the track become more regular and some low trees showed ahead of it, then they came up with a scrubby hedge, a bit of pasture, and a sheep-pen. The pasture showed more frequently. They passed a cottage with a smoking chimney. Just beyond it they went through a farmyard and through farm gates on to a narrow road. A mile further and they could see traffic passing on a hedgeless, straight, main road. It was the Norwich road. At the intersection a fingerpost said 'Latchford 3'. Deeming turned his head, showing his teeth.

'You'll be back for tea, screw,' he said. 'You like it I break two minutes between here and town?'

He didn't wait for an answer but wound the throttle three parts open. The machine soared off like a comet. They broke two minutes quite easily. Deeming tickered it in to Tony's park where the other machines were still lined up, placed it precisely in the line, shut it down and dropped the rest. Bixley strutted out from the doorway, stood looking ugly with his swollen upper lip.

'That was the coda, screw, that last bit,' Deeming said, swinging his goggles. 'Like I wanted you to have the full treatment, double-side L.P.'

His eyes were sparkling, he looked elated, he gave Bixley a flip on the shoulder.

'The screw just loved it,' he said. 'The screw just loved every minute.'

'Yuh, he must have done,' Bixley said thickly.

'Sure, he was crazy with it,' Deeming said. 'Like he

would have gone on touching till we ran out of gas. You underestimate the screw, Sid. You underestimate him bad. But he's wild there at the bottom of him, he's a wild, way-out screw. And like you'd do well to remember that, Sid, if you have any deals with him. It's crazy, the way he picks up tricks. You don't fool him for five minutes.'

'I'll remember it,' Bixley said.

'Yeah, he's mustard-sharp,' Deeming said. 'I wouldn't try pulling the wool with this screw. He's all round you. He digs everything.'

Gently took off the helmet and goggles, pulled his trousers out of his socks.

'Thanks for the entertainment,' he said. 'It makes a change from dull routine.'

'Any time,' Deeming said. 'We don't like screws having it dull.'

'Don't misunderstand me,' Gently said. 'Murder can never really be dull.'

He unlocked the Rover, got in, lit his pipe. They watched him silently. He drove away.

At the Sun it was later than teatime but his waitress fetched a tray for him in the lounge. He was surprisingly stiff from his bout of riding and his arm was aching where Hallman had punched it. He had the evening paper brought in. The Lister case had gone off the front page. The paper originated in Norwich and there was nothing in it about the business at Castlebridge. He ate his toasted teacakes sombrely, drank his tea, stared at the window.

He was back with his pipe when Setters came in. The local inspector looked relieved to see him.

'I've been trying to contact you all the afternoon,' he said. 'I couldn't seem to get a fix on you after you left Castlebridge. Then we got a motorist making a report about some dangerous driving in Five Mile Drove, and the car sounded a bit like yours, and you could have been there about then. Did you have any trouble?'

Gently grunted. 'Not to say trouble,' he replied. 'A little playfulness, perhaps, and some polished stage-management.'

'What this motorist reported didn't sound very playful.'

'It's a matter of taste,' Gently said. 'It might seem boisterous to some people.'

He gave Setters an account of the events of the day. Setters sat droopingly listening, dragging on a cigarette and flicking his nails. When Gently had finished Setters sat silent for some moments, then he said:

'It looks to me as though it's just the reefer-boys you've been having a tangle with.'

'That's how it looks,' Gently admitted.

'It looks to work this way,' Setters said. 'They knew you saw the collector at Castlebridge, so they aimed to confuse you, and lay on alibis, and take the juice out of you too. First there was two instead of one, then there was six instead of two. So you can't swear to any one of them, and one and all have got alibis. I didn't realize we'd got such clever bastards in Latchford.'

'But it wasn't necessary,' Gently said. 'That's the significant point. I didn't recognize the collector. All the play-acting was superfluous.'

'Bixley knew you'd suspect him,' Setters said. 'Maybe that's why he set it up. That and to make you look small, which he'd want to do to keep face.'

'But now I'm positive it was him,' Gently said, 'after a build-up like that. Or am I only supposed to be positive – was that the idea of it?'

'I don't get it,' Setters said. 'You're straining my poor provincial brain. But here's a hard fact I came to tell you – we found some sticks at Elton's place.'

He gave Gently a side glance.

'They were in the garden shed,' he said. 'There were five of them, in a box. A chocolate box. It's got no good prints on it.'

'Anything else?' Gently asked.

'Yes,' Setters said, 'from the Yard. They put a call through for you just this minute. That's why I came hunting you up.'

CHAPTER EIGHT

THEY WENT DOWN to Police H.Q. and Gently took the call in Setters' office. Pagram came on at the other end. He was eating something and talking with his mouth full.

'You've dropped some dynamite,' he said. 'Down in Narcotics you're the blue-eyed boy. That telephone number took them straight to the top man, a gent by the name of Leo Slavinovsky. They copped him bending with all the goods on him – and ten or a dozen of his associates. Don't mind me, I'm catching up, I'm having a picnic in the office.'

'Anything I can use?' Gently asked.

'I'd say it looks promising,' Pagram said. 'Slavinovsky's premises are in Gumbrill Street, Bethnal. Wasn't it Bethnal you had your eagle eye on?'

'Yes, Bethnal.' Gently nodded.

'Well, the results are still coming in. They've got some interesting records from Slavinovsky's safe which look like filling a few vacant cells. His set-up is definitely a Bethnal product. All the Cuthberts they've pulled in belong to that area. I've told them to check for connections with your wide boy at Latchford. I'm waiting now to hear from them. I'm eating canteen cheese rolls.'

'You'll have indigestion,' Gently said.

'A man must live,' said Pagram. 'Now you can hang up and let me finish. It's difficult to drink, eat, and talk.'

Gently hung up, made himself comfortable to wait for the call back. Setters came in with the box and reefers which he'd found at Elton's home. The box was a small one, a quarter-pound box, and of a different brand to those seized at Castlebridge. The reefers were of the same make. The box was empty except for the reefers.

Setters sat down beside the desk, lit a cigarette, drew heavily.

'I've been thinking,' he said. 'It was painful, but I did it.'

'About these?' Gently said.

Setters nodded, drew some more.

'It's having you with me,' he said. 'I can't keep it simple any longer. I keep being devious about everything, I want to come up with something clever. So though this rubs, I've got to say it. I think that crap is a plant.'

'Mmn,' Gently said. 'Did you talk to Maureen?'

'Yep,' Setters said, 'I talked to her. I think she knew Elton was smoking and I think she destroyed any sticks he left there. But I don't think she planted these. There's no single reason why she should. And she wouldn't have planted them in the shed, but in his bedroom somewhere. It's the shed angle that started me off, there's no lock on the shed. You've only to hop over the fence, sneak up the path, and open the door.'

'Was she there when you found them?' Gently asked.

'Yes,' Setters said. 'She was hanging around. I got the impression that she was surprised and didn't like it very much. But she wouldn't open up on it, other than swearing they weren't hers. I think they were planted and she's got a good idea about who did the planting.'

'Bixley,' Gently mused. 'Or one of his side-kicks.'

'From what you tell me,' Setters said, 'that would be the idea. I wouldn't know if his grapevine told him about what Greenstone gave us, but if it did this could be an attempt to fasten the reefer-passing on Elton. So like that it might not have been Elton who was sitting at the table with Betty Turner. It might have been Bixley, and he's got reasons for wanting to keep us from thinking that. Or maybe again he was just trying to make a scapegoat out of Elton, which attempt has now fallen through owing to what you saw at Castlebridge today.'

'Have you rung the hospital today?' Gently asked.

'Yes, twice,' Setters said. 'She's improving, she's got her eyes open. But she isn't talking yet.'

'It might not have been her Greenstone saw,' Gently said. 'It might not have been Bixley or Elton with her. All Greenstone was certain about was Lister and him taking the serviette.'

'And the sticks,' Setters said. 'Don't forget he took them.'

Gently nodded. 'It wasn't very gallant of him to take his fiancée's supply of reefers.'

'Meaning?' Setters asked.

'Just a point,' Gently said. 'Because it might not have been Betty Turner who Greenstone saw. Perhaps Lister was deeper in this than we thought. Perhaps he took the reefers because the girl couldn't pay for them. There may be an angle we haven't got on to why he was ridden off the road.'

Setters looked doubtful. 'I like it simple,' he said. 'That's my natural-born instinct. If there was something else we'd have got a smell of it beyond all this surmising. We're getting smoke blown in our eyes with this dope-peddling business. The fact is Elton had a motive, and I don't see where anyone else has.'

'Mmn.' Gently conceded the point. 'He's certainly in it up to his eyeballs. Leach, the man they've arrested over at Castlebridge, was trying to help me keep it with Elton.'

'You think he was lying?'

'Like a trooper.'

'It might have been the truth,' Setters said.

'He was lying,' Gently affirmed. 'Though it may have been only to oblige a customer. Bixley's alibi isn't cast iron. It's just on the cards he caught up with Lister.'

'But what was his motive?' Setters asked.

Gently shrugged. 'There's none to date.'

'I don't like it,' Setters said. 'I wish to Christ we could pick up Elton.'

He lit another cigarette from his butt, smoked silently for a while. The station routine went on outside, voices, feet tramping, a telephone bell. Gently sat poring over the box and reefers, his eyes narrowed and unshifting.

Setters sat hugging a bony knee, he'd got the visitor's chair, it wasn't comfortable.

'There's Dicky Deeming,' Setters pondered. 'Do you think he knows what goes on?'

Gently smiled at the box. 'He plays the big brother,' he said.

'He's got influence with them,' Setters said. 'You've only to talk to them to find that out. I don't like him, I don't like his influence, but he never bothers us.'

'He's their high priest,' Gently said.

'Yes?' Setters said. 'What would that be?'

'Just high priest,' Gently said, 'the one who gives them the law.'

'This jeebie stuff?' Setters asked.

Gently nodded. 'That's it. It's Dicky who's spread the gospel in Latchford. It came to Latchford with Dicky.'

'I knew I didn't like him,' Setters said. 'I knew there had to be a reason. Hell, I'll make it tough for Dicky – fetching that stinking stuff in here!'

No.' Gently shook his head. 'That's the wrong sort of treatment. If you make a martyr out of Dicky you'll play right into his hands. The cult has got a religious twist, it'll flourish on persecution. So don't knock it, don't push it, just ignore it where you can.'

'Pushing reefers,' Setters said. 'Riding bikes like madmen.'

'That's where you don't ignore it,' Gently said. 'That's where you clamp down hard. But don't touch Dicky for the moment, let him amuse himself with me. His influence has got a credit side. He tries to keep his flock from being rowdy.'

Setters sniffed. 'Are you on to him for something?'

'I'm not quite certain,' Gently said. 'He's in this business, and yet he's detached from it. But he's certainly on to me.'

'You mean it was him who set it up today.'

'He played a big part in it,' Gently said. 'But whether it was for devilment or for a reason is something I haven't settled yet. Perhaps tomorrow's paper will tell us.'

'Yeah, perhaps,' said Setters sourly.

'He's a beautiful rider,' Gently said. 'He's got courage, a lot of that.'

The phone jangled. He picked it up. After a moment, Pagram came on.

'This may seem a bit involved,' Pagram began. 'But it could be what you're after. Does the name of Waters mean anything to you?'

'Nothing whatever,' Gently said.

'Well, one of the chummies we've caught is called Waters and his mother was a Lemon.'

'A Lemon?' Gently queried.

'Yes,' Pagram said. 'You still sound vague. But Cissie Lemon was his mother and she's got a sister called Ruby. I've got some notes here from a P.C. Noble who swears he knows what he's talking about.'

'Go on,' said Gently patiently.

'We're coming to it,' Pagram said. 'Now Cissie's sister married a van driver, and this is where we get the connection. The van driver's name was Arthur Bixley. I rather think he's Sidney Bixley's father.'

'That's the one,' Gently said.

'I thought it could be,' Pagram said. 'So like that

Sidney is a cousin of Waters', and Waters is a member of the Slavinovsky gang. Is that what you wanted?'

'Roughly speaking,' Gently said.

'You were right about the cheese rolls,' Pagram said. 'I'm having one analysed down in the lab.'

Gently laid the phone on its rest. He pondered dreamily for a moment.

'Can we get a search warrant done quickly?' he asked. Setters nodded. 'I've got one on tap.'

'Right,' Gently said. 'We're going to search Bixley's house. And while we're at it, I think we'd better have Bixley picked up for questioning.'

The Bixleys lived in a terrace house in Breck Hill Road, which lay on the furthest edge of the New Town Area. Though the houses were terraced they were neatly crow-stepped up a gentle rise and this gave to each one a faint air of individuality. The Bixleys lived at fifty-seven, more than halfway up. A light showed in their kitchen, which was situated at the front. Gently rang, and the door was opened by a bow-shouldered man in shirtsleeves. He looked startled to find three men on his doorstep.

'Yes,' he said. 'What are you after?' He kept the door on the balance.

'Police,' Gently said. 'Are you Mr Bixley?'

The bow-shouldered man seemed uncertain.

'What are you after?' he repeated. 'If you want to talk to Sid, he isn't in just now.'

'We have a search warrant,' Gently said, producing it. 'I tell you Sid's not here,' said the man.

'It's made out for the premises,' Gently said. 'We'll have to come in, Mr Bixley.'

The man frowned at it, looked puzzled, then backed away from the door. Gently entered with Setters and Ralphs. They stood in a small hall which contained the staircase.

'You'll have to wait a mo',' the man said. 'Maybe Ruby ain't respectable.'

He stuck his head round the kitchen door.

'Right you are,' he said.

They followed him into the kitchen. It was a small room with a coke-fired boiler. It contained a dining table, two old armchairs, three straight-back chairs and a television set. From one of the armchairs a woman had risen and she was hastily dragging on a skirt. She stared angrily at the intruders, shoving in her blouse with stumpy fingers.

'Arter,' she said. 'What do you mean letting these men in here, Arter?'

Arter wagged his bow-shoulders. 'I couldn't help it, Ruby,' he said. 'They got a warrant and everything. I told them Sid wasn't in.'

'That ain't no reason,' Ruby said. 'You don't have to let them in like this.'

She was a big, formidable woman with arms like pale, freckled hams. She was a good deal larger than her husband. Her husband had a sad, colourless face.

Gently said:

'I'm afraid we must inconvenience you, Mrs Bixley. We've reason to think that your son is concealing prohibited drugs in this house. We've come to search it, also I'd like to ask you some questions about him. The questions can wait, if you like, till you've watched us make the search.'

'Ho,' she said. 'Well, you put it like a gentleman, don't you?'

She eased the blouse out a little, buttoned it across her straining brassiere.

'You won't find nothing here,' she said, 'prying into all our little affairs. But you can look, that's all right. Arter can see you don't pinch nothing.'

Setters with Ralphs made a businesslike beginning in the kitchen, but apart from the built-in cupboards and a small pantry it contained few likely places of concealment. Setters poked the two armchairs and turned them over to inspect the springs. Ralphs moved a rug, trod heavily about the stained boards which formed the floor. Mrs Bixley watched them aggressively. Arter rolled himself a fag.

'That's about it,' Setters said, after stirring in a flour-bin and replacing it.

Trailing Arter behind them, they went out to continue next door. Mrs Bixley repossessed an arm-chair, jerked a thumb at the other one.

'You better sit down,' she said to Gently. 'Nothing like making yourselves at home. And there ain't much I can tell you about our Sid what you don't know already. You're the Yard one, ain't you?'

Gently nodded, sat himself.

'Thought you were,' said Mrs Bixley. 'You got more savvy about you than them two. It ain't the same down here like it is back home, they just ain't got the know. Now what's our Sid been up to this time?'

'What we told you,' Gently said. 'And you know about it, don't you, Mrs Bixley?'

'If I did I'd be a fool to let on, wouldn't I?' she retorted. 'But I ain't saying I'm so blooming innocent. I've seen him have them reefers around. But cor love us, I ask you, what's a thing like that to make a fuss over?'

'When have you seen him have them around?'

'When?' She made her eyes round. 'Do us a favour, I can't remember the ins and outs like that. But I've caught him smoking one sometimes – pooh, I can't stand that stink! I told him I wouldn't have it in here, he'd have to do it somewhere else.'

'You didn't want to know where he'd got them?'

'Don't be silly,' she said. 'Where do kids always get them from – off each other, that's where.'

'They don't make them themselves, Mrs Bixley.'

'Didn't say they did, did I? One of them buys them in a pub or a street corner or somewhere. You know how it is. They will go for these things. Me, I tried one when I was that age, it made me spew something rotten.'

'How many have you seen him have at one time?'

'Only the one,' said Mrs Bixley. 'Then it was the stink what made me notice it, I'd come in here and niff the stink.'

'You haven't seen him have a box of them?'

'No I haven't,' she said.

'Have you seen him with boxes of Melton chocolates?'

'What, Sid?' she said. 'Do us a favour.'

Gently paused, let her think about that for a moment.

In the next room they could hear the squeak of furniture being moved on linoleum. Mrs Bixley sat saggingly with her slippered feet placed apart, her elbows dug into the arms of the chair, her chin jutted out towards him.

'How often do you hear from your sister, Cissie?' Gently asked.

Her eyes jumped at him. Well,' she said, 'we know a few things, don't we? And what's Cissie got to do with it?'

'Have you seen her lately?' Gently asked.

'Not since we come here,' said Mrs Bixley. 'And that was two years in August. Her and me don't get on since that business about Mum's furniture. Took the blinking lot, she did. And the sewing machine. And the canary.'

'Too bad,' Gently said. 'When did you last see her son?'

'Him,' Mrs Bixley said scornfully. 'We don't have no truck with young Perce. A proper tulip he is, he takes after his old man. Our Sid would make two of him. Perce is a nasty bit of work.'

'Were Sid and he pals?'

'Yers, likely,' said Mrs Bixley. 'Well they were in a sort of way, when we was home in Bethnal. I reckon it was Perce who was to blame when Sid had his little bit of trouble. Led my boy on, he did. Sid's all right if he's left alone.'

'How did Perce lead him into trouble?' Gently asked.

Mrs Bixley rounded her eyes. 'Go on,' she said. 'You know about that. You can't tell a copper nothing about a boy who's been in trouble.'

'I'd like you to tell me,' Gently said.

'Here, what's this?' Mrs Bixley demanded. 'All that there is over and done with, you can't pin that on Sid again.'

'Sid was a gang-boy,' Gently said. 'Was it Perce who introduced him to the gang?'

'That's as may be,' said Mrs Bixley. 'Just you leave Perce out of this.'

'But that was what you meant, wasn't it?'

'Suppose it was.' Mrs Bixley glared. 'That's finished with, that is. Why do you think we come out this way? So's we could get Sid away from them lot, that's the blinking reason for it.'

'Have you heard of a man called Leo Slavinovsky?'

'Yes,' she said. 'So has everyone in Bethnal.'

'In connection with Perce?' Gently asked.

'Never you mind,' Mrs Bixley said.

'He ran that gang, didn't he?' Gently said. 'He ran it when Sid was one of the gang. He planned the job when Sid was arrested. He was the big noise in Bethnal.'

Mrs Bixley dug at the chair-arms. 'I ain't saying nothing about him,' she said. 'It's up to you coppers to handle blokes like Leo. Just don't ask me questions about him.'

'He was arrested today,' Gently said.

Mrs Bixley said nothing.

'Perce was arrested too,' Gently said. 'On a charge of trafficking in reefers.'

'Sid—' Mrs Bixley began. She stopped.

'Sid's in it, too, isn't he?' Gently said. 'We've found a depot for the reefers over at Castlebridge. Sid's been the one who's distributed them here.'

She jammed her lips tight shut, sat perfectly still. A tramp of feet overhead indicated that Setters was in the bedrooms. They could hear drawers opened and closed, the faint creaking of bed-springs, then Arter's whining voice as he answered a question. The expression on Mrs Bixley's face grew tighter and tighter.

'Surely,' Gently said, 'you wondered where Sid got his money from? How he paid for that bike and his expensive riding clothes? He doesn't work very often from what I've heard, yet he acts as though he's got plenty of money to throw about.'

'I give him some,' she said.

'How much, Mrs Bixley?'

'How should I know?' she said. 'I give him some now and then.'

'How much does your husband earn?'

'I got some money of Mum's,' she said.

'You keep it in the bank, Mrs Bixley?'

'You rotten bastard,' she said.

Gently shrugged, went on listening to the sounds upstairs. A muffled voice from far above suggested that Ralphs was in the loft. Then there was a clink of metal as somebody uncovered the flush cistern, and finally steps on the stairs and a draught from the back door.

'You stinking lot,' said Mrs Bixley. 'Coming in here like this. We ain't got nothing to hide. Sid wouldn't keep nothing here. But you rotten bastards come nosing in here as though we'd pinched the Crown Jewels. You rotten sods. You rotten sods. We come here to keep Sid away from them.'

'You knew he was up to something,' Gently said.

'I didn't know nothing,' said Mrs Bixley. 'He got a job too, and all. It was going to be different up here. And Arter, he's doing all right. We got the telly and a washer. And Sid worked for a bit. I reckoned it was going to be all right.'

'How long did he work?' Gently asked.

'That don't matter,' said Mrs Bixley. 'He got a job, he did, and he worked for a bit. I didn't like it when he slung it, but Sid had always been restless. And things was going all right. We been up here two years.'

'Did he get letters from Perce?' Gently asked.

Mrs Bixley shook her head.

'Has he been back to Bethnal since he came here?'

'Once,' she said. 'He went to Cissie's.'

'When would that have been, Mrs Bixley?'

'Oh, a long time ago,' she said.

'About when he gave up his job?' Gently asked.

She dug at the chair, her mouth drooping.

'And when was that?' Gently asked.

She was staring at the floor as though she didn't hear him.

Time passed. Setters came back. He made a negative gesture with his hands. Ralphs and Arter came in behind him, the latter with a yellowish tab-end gummed to his lip. Gently got up.

'That's that,' he said. 'Sorry we had to pay you a visit.'

'I'll bet you are,' Arter said. 'All fun and games for you, this is.'

'I've spoken to your wife,' Gently said. 'I'm afraid we'll be taking your son in for questioning.'

'Much obliged, I'm sure,' Arter said. 'That'll be very nice for Sid.'

Mrs Bixley didn't say anything, kept staring at the floor.

They sat in the car, Setters with Gently, Ralphs silent in the rear. Setters' hands were very dirty and he'd picked up some rust on his trousers.

'The First and Last,' Setters said slowly.

'It's a good bet,' Gently said.

'But they'll be moved by now,' Setters said. 'If Bixley's as smart as we think he is. So where would he move them from there? Where would he think we wouldn't look? Or is he out of stock now, owing to a hitch in supplies this morning?'

'He won't be out of stock,' Gently said. 'He wasn't working hand to mouth. There'll be a hoard of the stuff somewhere, you can put your promotion on that. We'll have to check the First and Last because it stands out a mile – and because chummies are sometimes stupid. Though I don't think this chummie is.'

He told Setters what he had elicited from Mrs Bixley about Bixley and Waters, about the coincidence between Bixley's London visit and the giving-up of his employment. Setters kept nodding sapiently.

'You're doing well down here,' he said. 'I wish it was getting us closer to Lister, but either way you're doing well.'

'Bixley is close to Lister, very close,' Gently said.

'Elton paddled in Lister's blood,' Setters said. 'You can't get much closer than that.'

'Think,' Gently said, 'think a moment. Lister was killed on the way back from Leach's café. Bixley was there. He was collecting his chocolates. And on the way back from there, Lister is killed. Is it just one of those strange coincidences, or is it a tie-up we can't overlook?'

Setters thought. 'It's a tie-up,' he admitted grudgingly. 'But don't forget that Elton is right in the middle of it. He didn't love Lister. He was a side-kick of Bixley's. And he was there where he could do the job, which you haven't proved that Bixley was.'

'Forget Elton a moment,' Gently said. 'Think of Bixley and the chocolates.'

Setters nodded again. 'I begin to see where you're getting,' he said. 'You think there was trouble over those chocolates. You think maybe Lister half-inched them. Then could be Bixley busted him off, trying to stop him to get them back. Is that the angle with Bixley?'

'It suggests itself,' Gently said.

'And Elton maybe took a side road?'

'Elton was there,' Gently said. 'Elton was there because you proved it and because the facts all prove it. But the part he played in what happened is something we still have to guess at.'

'Bixley had a passenger,' Setters said. 'And a passenger is a witness. And Bixley was a quarter of an hour behind. I can't see Bixley doing the busting. But Elton didn't have a passenger and Elton left right after Lister, so if this chocolates angle holds I'd say that Elton was told to recover them. Which gives me another motive for Elton. And lets Bixley out of the picture.'

'You're missing something,' Gently said.

'I'm doing my best,' Setters said.

'Bixley is an expert rider,' Gently said. 'I'm told locally he's the mostest.'

'Yeah,' Setters said. 'So what does that prove? That Elton bungled it when he busted-off Lister. I'd say he did it trying to stop him and not knowing a better way to do it. And that still adds up to Elton having done it, whether by accident or with malice aforethought. And I like that accident angle best, I never could see Elton as a deliberate killer.'

'Nor could I,' Gently said. 'Especially with Betty Turner on Lister's pillion.' He pulled the starter, brushed the gear in. 'We'll get a warrant for the First and Last,' he said. 'Also one for Mr Deeming's rooms, just in case Mr Deeming is being quixotic.'

CHAPTER NINE

THEY DROVE BACK to Police H.Q. Bixley had been cooling his heels there for an hour. He'd been picked up straight away at the First and Last café where two detective constables had found him engaged in the usual jukebox session. Deeming wasn't among those present and there had been a little trouble. Bixley had collected a black eye to add to his thick lip. He had been abusive as well as violent. One of the detective constables was attending him.

'A pity,' Setters observed, 'we drew a blank at his house.'

He got on the phone to the local magistrate to request the new warrants. Gently lit his pipe, sat smoking, drawing patterns on Setters' desk-pad. Ralphs, who had missed his tea, had departed to make a quick meal.

'It's going to be tricky,' Setters said. 'If we keep drawing a blank. We've got no handle for Bixley, he can laugh in our face.'

'Yes,' Gently said. He kept drawing on the pad.

'We can't hold him,' Setters continued. 'And it would be a good idea to hold him.'

'Very good,' Gently agreed.

'So what's the routine?' Setters said.

'I'll have a chat with him,' Gently said. 'Now. I'll leave you to look after the searches.'

'Hmn,' Setters said. 'Well, if you think it will do any good. But me, I'd sooner have a charge to throw at him before I tried to go to work. But then, I'm just a bucolic. I'll leave you Baynes to sit in.'

'Is he a shorthand writer?' Gently asked.

'Yeah,' Setters said. 'Expecting a confession?'

'Window-dressing,' Gently said. 'It never hurts to dress the window.'

Setters went out to collect his warrants and sent in Detective Constable Baynes. Baynes was a heavy-featured man with a fresh complexion and slow, blue eyes. He had a bruise on the side of his chin. He grinned sheepishly when Gently noticed it.

'Chummie copped me a fourpenny one, sir,' he said. 'Didn't take to the idea of coming down here.'

Gently gave him his instructions, sent him to fetch in Bixley. While he was gone Gently placed a chair in the centre of the floor in front of the desk. Setters had got an adjustable desk-lamp. Gently trained it on the chair. Then he switched off the overhead light and retired to the gloom behind the desk.

A few moments later he heard Baynes's footsteps marching briskly down the corridor. The door was tapped and thrown open and Baynes clicked his heels.

'Bixley, sir.'

He gave Bixley a nudge which sent him staggeringly into the office. Bixley nearly collided with the chair. He stood holding the back of it, blinking furiously.

'Sit down, Bixley,' Gently said.

'Like what's this about?' Bixley began.

Baynes laid two large hands on Bixley's shoulders and sat him down on the chair.

'Lock the door, please,' Gently said.

Baynes made a business of locking the door. In point of fact there wasn't a key, but Baynes made a convincing sound with the latch.

'Now if you'll bring your book to the desk here,' Gently said, 'I'd like a transcript of Bixley's answers.'

Baynes took a chair to the end of the desk, scuffed through a notebook, laid out three pencils.

'Good,' Gently said.

'Like what's going on?' Bixley broke out again.

Baynes immediately seized a pencil and commenced a ferocious scribble.

'I think,' Gently said, 'you'd better listen to me and simply answer my questions, Bixley. That way you won't go saying things you wouldn't like to see in a report afterwards. Do you understand me?'

Bixley glared at the light. His pupils were contracted and he was sweating.

'Like tell me, screw,' he said, 'and tell me straight. What's this jazz all about?'

'Take it down,' said Gently unnecessarily.

'Take nothing down!' Bixley bawled. 'I ain't done nothing and like you know it, so why am I hung up in here?'

'Have you finished?' Gently asked.

'No I haven't,' Bixley said. 'I'm asking you, screw, and I want an answer. You ain't got no right to keep me down here.'

'When you have finished,' Gently said, 'I'll do the talking if you don't mind, Bixley. And just remember that this is a police station. It'll be to your advantage not to forget it.'

Bixley swore at him obscenely.

'Take it down,' Gently said.

Baynes went scribbling down the page, flipped it over and scribbled some more.

'Now,' Gently said. 'Is that all?'

It apparently was. Bixley only glared.

'Right,' Gently said. 'You're being sensible. Let's see if you can answer a few questions. Where were you this morning?'

'You know where I was,' Bixley snarled.

'I think I do,' Gently said. 'You were in Castlebridge, weren't you?'

'Like I wasn't, then,' Bixley said. 'I wasn't nowhere near Castlebridge. I was out riding like you said. And nobody can't prove different.'

'Where were you riding?' Gently asked.

'I was out on the heath,' Bixley said.

'Where out on the heath?'

'Just out on the heath,' Bixley said.

'Then you couldn't have been recognized,' Gently said, 'by a man you talked to in Castlebridge?'

'I wasn't there,' Bixley said.

'Make sure you've got that answer,' Gently said to Baynes.

He gave Baynes time for plenty of scribbling.

'Do you know a man named Leach?' he asked.

'Like suppose I do,' Bixley said. 'He only keeps a café, don't he?'

'He used to keep one,' Gently said. 'Just at this moment he's keeping a cell warm. He was arrested at about nine a.m. this morning, around the time when you weren't in Castlebridge.'

'So what's that to do with me?' Bixley said.

'We've been asking him questions,' Gently said. 'And we've been going through some of his records. Did you know that Leach kept records?'

'He wouldn't have said nothing,' Bixley said.

'He,' Gently said, 'couldn't help it. And he wasn't quite quick enough hiding his records. I got hold of a notebook I shouldn't have seen.'

'He's a stupid git,' Bixley said.

'He knew quite a lot about Tuesday.'

'He didn't know—' Bixley began. He stopped, tried to pierce the haze beside the lamp.

'What didn't he know?' Gently asked. 'That some of his chocolates had gone astray?'

'Like I don't know what you're talking about,' Bixley said. 'What's this jazz about chocolates?'

Gently turned in Baynes's direction. Baynes's pencil scuttered, halted with a dab.

'Yuh, what's it about?' Bixley demanded. 'I don't know nothing about his chocolates. Like he used to give chocolates for prizes, he did. Put a spot on someone, that sort of action.'

'And you used to win them,' Gently said.

'Yuh,' Bixley said. 'I sometimes won one.'

'Every Tuesday,' Gently said. 'Including the Tuesday of last week. Only last Tuesday you had some trouble with them. Maybe Lister thought it was his turn for a prize.'

Bixley was silent. He kept blinking in the lamp-glare. His eyes had puckers round them. The puckers were twitching. At first his hands had been clenched into fists but now they lay hot and thick-looking on his knees. He opened his mouth and closed it again.

'You'd been a little careless,' Gently said. 'You put those chocolates on a table for a moment. Then when you looked for them they weren't there. And Lister wasn't there. They'd gone off together. And you're telling me Leach didn't know about that?'

'He didn't know nothing about—' Bixley jerked.

'Not about Lister being the culprit?'

'He was bleeding guessing!' Bixley said.

'If he said that Lister had taken the chocolates?'

'Yuh – no!' Bixley said. 'I keep telling you I don't know nothing about it. I didn't have no chocolates pinched, nor nothing like that happened at all.'

'You collected a box on Tuesday, didn't you?'

'No,' Bixley said. 'I never did.'

'So nobody could have seen you with a box?'

'It ain't a crime, is it?' Bixley said. 'Being given a box of chocolates?'

'But you had one?'

'All right!' he said. 'So Leachy give me a box of chocolates.'

'And you gave Leachy forty quid.'

'No!' Bixley shouted. 'I never.'

'Even though he says you did?'

'The bloody rat!' Bixley said.

'Verbatim,' Gently said to Baynes. 'I don't want any of this lost.'

He sat back in the chair, a dark presence, concealedly studying the sweating Bixley. Bixley was breathing very heavily, he'd stopped trying to see Gently through the light.

'Of course,' Gently said smoothly, 'you'd want those chocolates back again, wouldn't you? After you'd spent forty quid on them and had a chocolate-monopoly here in Latchford. You could afford the forty quid, but not Lister muscling in on your racket. So you had to get that box back from him. I can see how important that was.'

'I didn't go after him,' Bixley said. 'I got an alibi, I have.'

'Don't interrupt,' Gently said. 'Let's do some thinking about this, shall we? There's Elton, he left soon after Lister, he could have caught him up easily. And no doubt Elton had his reasons for doing what you might ask of him. When you've acquired a taste for chocolates you have to toe the line, don't you? So you might have sent Elton after Lister. It seems a reasonable assumption.'

'I tell you I never—!' Bixley howled.

No,' Gently said. 'I'm coming to that. You didn't send Elton after Lister because you couldn't trust him to do the job. He'd have to stop Lister as well as catch him, and after stopping him he'd have to get the chocolates. But Elton wasn't an expert rider, nor was he a very formidable person. Not like you yourself, Bixley. You fit the bill much better.'

Bixley was halfway to his feet. Gently crashed his fist on the desk.

'Keep your seat, please,' he said mildly. 'We're coming to the interesting part now.'

'But it's a bleeding lie!' Bixley shouted.

'You'll kindly sit down, all the same.'

'I got my alibi!' Bixley shouted.

'You had fifteen minutes,' Gently said.

Bixley sank on the chair again, his cheeks flushed, his eyes staring. He leaned forward towards the desk as though he'd got a stitch in his stomach.

'Fifteen minutes,' Gently continued. 'That sounds a lot on a fast motorcycle. But you can ride a motorcycle fast or slowly, you aren't compelled to go at full throttle. Then sometimes you stop to pick up petrol, or maybe to buy some fish and chips. Or you might have a girlfriend on the back who wasn't so keen on mad driving. There's one or a number of possible reasons why fifteen minutes wasn't a safe margin – not for Lister, that is. It might have looked safe enough as an alibi. So, you gave him that fifteen minutes. The way you ride, you could make it up. Then, if as was likely, you had trouble with him, you had your alibi ready to hand.'

'I tell you it's crazy!' Bixley bawled. 'I never thought nothing like that at all. You're making it up, that's what you're doing. I couldn't never catch him after quarter of an hour.'

'You ride a new Matchless six-fifty,' Gently said.

'So what if I do!' Bixley shouted.

'Lister's bike was an Aerial five hundred, two years old. And he was carrying a passenger.'

'But I didn't go after him!' Bixley shouted.

'I think you did,' Gently said. 'And I think you caught him at Five Mile Drove and you didn't care how you stopped him. Elton was there. You passed Elton. Elton was the witness and Elton's missing. He saw you ride those two off the road, and stop, and take that box from the wreckage. And you made Elton swear to keep his mouth shut, or he'd finish up like Lister. And when it looked as though we'd pin it on Elton, you put Elton in a place where he couldn't talk.'

Bixley rocked back in the chair, his face greyish. His eyes were straining at their sockets.

'I never,' he croaked, 'I never! You'll never hang that one on me, screw.'

Gently's fist smashed the desk again.

'What happened to Elton, Bixley?' he said.

'He's gone, cleared out,' Bixley gabbled. 'I don't know nothing. I didn't do it.'

'Where's he gone?'

'I don't know,' Bixley said.

'I think you do.'

'No,' Bixley said, 'no.'

'He's not very far from here, is he, Bixley?'

'I don't know,' Bixley said. 'I don't know. I don't know.'

'He's not very far, but he's very quiet.'

'I don't know nothing,' Bixley said. 'I don't know nothing.'

'It'll come to you later,' Gently said. 'Now we'll get on to Leo. Leo Slavinovsky.'

* * *

Baynes scribbled away industriously, dabbed, and stopped. After the scratching of his pencil one heard nothing but Bixley's breathing. The room seemed heavy round the directed light, a place of infinite insulation. Bixley sat in the light under the weight of the room like an illuminated object on a slide. From the shadows eyes examined him, applied a stimulus, made a note.

'When did you last see Leo?' Gently asked.

'Who – what Leo?' Bixley said hoarsely.

'Little Leo back in Bethnal. The big brain,' Gently said.

'I don't know any Leo,' Bixley said.

'He'd be hurt,' Gently said. 'I'm sure he had big hopes for you, Bixley. You were an up-an-coming gang-boy.'

'I ain't had nothing to do with him,' Bixley said. 'I never had. I don't know him. That job I was pulled for I did on me own, I don't know no Leo.'

'Your cousin knows him,' Gently said.

'I ain't seen my cousin, not since I come here.'

'Once,' Gently said, 'you saw him. About the time when work was getting too heavy for you.'

'That's a bloody lie,' Bixley said.

'Is your mother a liar?' Gently asked.

'She – she's a stupid so-and-so,' Bixley said. 'She got things mixed, that's all it is.'

'Percy Waters was arrested today.'

'So what?' Bixley said. 'He's another stupid.'

'Leo Slavinovsky was arrested today.'

'I tell you I don't know nothing about him.'

'Listen,' Gently said. 'I'm going to do some more thinking.'

'I've had enough of this!' Bixley yelped. 'You bleeding let me out of here. I ain't done nothing, you know I ain't. I got alibis and you can't touch me. I ain't going to sit here having it shot at me, I bleeding ain't. You let me out!'

'But you aren't going anywhere,' Gently said.

'I'll get a lawyer!' Bixley shouted.

'You'll be good business, too,' Gently said. 'Only right at this moment you're going to listen to me.'

'I bloody won't listen!'

'You'd better,' Gently said. 'Otherwise you won't know what to tell your lawyer.'

Bixley swore.

'Are we going too fast?' Gently asked Baynes.

Baynes shook his head. 'I can do a hundred and sixty, sir,' he said. 'We've got a special set of lettergrams for use with swear words. Very useful they are in this line of business.'

'Stop me if you're getting behind,' Gently said.

'Yes, sir. But I've had no trouble so far.'

Bixley sat trembling, worrying his thick lip. There was sweat on his cheeks, down each side of his chin.

'Right,' Gently said. 'Are you listening to what I say to you, Bixley?'

'I ought to have done you,' Bixley muttered. 'Christ, if I'd only done you, screw.'

'You're in trouble enough,' Gently said. 'Another thick lip wouldn't have helped you. So let's do some thinking about Leo and Cousin Perce.'

Bixley moaned, said nothing.

'I think you heard from Perce,' Gently said. 'I think

he told you he'd got something for you and that you'd better look him up. So you did, you went to Bethnal, you saw Perce and Leo. You heard that business was flourishing with Leo and that he was planning a little expansion. He was going to put Leach in Castlebridge to run a chocolate depot there – it was a good place for pushing chocolates, a university town. And Leo had remembered his old gang-boy who'd gone to live here in Latchford, and Leo thought that perhaps Latchford could absorb a few chocolates, too. So he proposed that you took care of that district for him, drawing your supplies from Leach on some weekly excursion to Castlebridge. And you liked that proposal, didn't you, Bixley? It might have been made to measure for you. It meant a return to the easy money you'd been missing – and it flattered you, Leo choosing you for a job like that.'

Bixley croaked: It's bloody lies, bloody lies, that's what it is.'

'Leo and Perce,' Gently said, 'haven't got much left to lie about now.'

'I only know what you tell me,' Bixley said. 'I know screws. Bloody liars. It's all lies, every bit of it.'

'I wouldn't,' Gently said, 'back that horse, if I were you. We didn't guess about Leo and his trade in chocolates. Suppose you start brightening up a little, give us a little cooperation. You're on your own now, Bixley. All your pals are inside.'

'They ain't my pals. I didn't never know them.'

'Where did Lister come into it?' Gently asked.

'I don't know about Lister.'

'Why did he whip that box of chocolates?'

'I don't know nothing about that,' Bixley said. 'It's lies, all lies.'

'We're out looking for your chocolate-store, Bixley.'

'Yuh,' Bixley said. 'Bloody look for it.'

'We'll find it, too,' Gently said.

'Yuh,' Bixley said. 'I ain't got one.'

'Not at Tony's,' Gently said.

'I ain't got one,' Bixley repeated.

'Not at Dicky's,' Gently said.

'You've a bleeding hope.' Bixley said.

'How will you manage without chocolates?' Gently said.

'Crap on your chocolates,' Bixley said.

'You've smoked your last one,' Gently said. 'It's going to be tough if you've been at them heavy.'

'I don't smoke sticks,' Bixley said.

'Oh, yes,' Gently said. 'I think you do.'

'I ain't never had nothing to do with them.'

'We'll see,' Gently said. 'Your pockets will tell us.'

Bixley got unsteadily to his feet. 'They bloody won't,' he said. 'They won't, because I ain't got none. So you can search as much as you like.'

'You'll let me search you?' Gently asked.

'Yuh,' Bixley said. 'You search me.'

'You can sit down again,' Gently said. 'That's all I want to know for the moment.'

'I tell you you can search me,' Bixley said.

Gently ignored him, turned to Baynes.

'Go and look in the waiting room,' he told him. 'Bring back anything interesting you find there.'

Baynes nodded, got up, departed. Bixley came up to the desk, put his hands on it.

'I'll get you for this,' he said. 'If it's the last bloody thing. I'll get you, screw. I don't care if I swing for it.'

'You've been watching too much TV,' Gently said.

'I mean it,' Bixley said. 'I'm going to get you. I mean it.'

He kept standing there, leaning, glaring at Gently.

'I mean it,' he kept saying. 'I mean it, I mean it.'

Baynes returned, carrying in his hand a cigarette case which combined a petrol-lighter. His hands were sooty and there was soot on the case.

'It was stuffed up the chimney of the stove,' he said. 'He'd had the soot-door off. It's a finger-screw job.'

Gently took the lighter. It was flamboyantly engraved: S.A.B. He sprang it open. It contained twenty-three of the reefers.

'Somebody else's?' He asked Bixley.

'I mean it,' said Bixley. 'I mean it.'

'And I mean this,' Gently said. 'I'm charging you with having possession of prohibited drugs. You don't need to say anything in answer to the charge.'

'I ain't saying anything,' Bixley said. 'Not nothing at all.'

Nobody was saying anything. Gently rang the Yard again and got in touch with the Chief Inspector in charge of the Slavinovsky interrogations. There they were having an all-night session, but it hadn't got them much further. Slavinovsky himself, a Polish Jew, hadn't breathed a word in five hours. Some of the smaller fry had squeaked and a few more arrests had been made.

Two experts were working on the code in which Slavinovsky kept his records.

'We're getting the impression,' the C.I. told Gently 'that there were other depots like the one in Castlebridge. But we still haven't got a clue as to how the stuff was coming in. It's Cyprus hemp we seized in Bethnal, we're checking all the known channels. I think Slavinovsky's building his hopes on us not cracking the code.'

'Has Percy Waters talked?' Gently inquired.

'Not as yet,' the C.I. replied. 'Pagram briefed me on your interest and I'm doing my best to get you something. The trouble is, we want everything quickly. You understand that, don't you? Time's against us, we have to keep plugging away at the main issues.'

'I've got a murder at this end,' Gently said.

'We're doing our best,' said the C.I. 'The moment Bixley's name comes up I'll give you a ring at Latchford.'

It was just after ten when Setters got back, dirtier than ever and looking bushed. He dropped on the visitor's chair in the office, lit a cigarette, and took several deep drags.

'Nothing,' he said. 'Just the fun.'

'How did Deeming take it?' Gently asked.

'Dicky,' said Setters, 'played records, did some typing, made light conversation. I've had a basinful of Dicky. I was bloody polite to him. Bloody.'

'And Tony?' Gently asked.

'He was throwing a fit the whole time. And we had the jeebies on our necks, though they were quiet, for a change.'

Gently nodded, told Setters how his interrogation had gone. Setters sat very quiet when he heard that Bixley had been charged.

'Yep,' he said at last. 'That was good. Me, I'd have searched him and risked the rap. Or maybe I wouldn't, I'd have fallen down on it. I don't aspire to such class.'

Gently grinned. 'I can take it,' he said.

Setters grinned too. 'I'm whacked,' he said. 'Just reprimand me and let me go home. I need a bath to set me up.'

But he got on the phone and made the arrangements for Bixley's appearance in court in the morning.

Gently drove him home, to Ashgrove Road, drove to the Sun, parked, smoked a last pipe.

CHAPTER TEN

THE COURTROOM AT Latchford was in the medieval guildhall, and courts had been held there since 1452. Like all the oldest buildings in Latchford it was built of dressed flint and Caen stone. The Caen stone had been brought up the River Latch, which flowed into the Ouse, and so into the Wash. The flint was the native stone of the country and had been the wealth of the aboriginal tribes. Thus the pale stone was a modern innovation in the time scheme of Latchford, a mere frame, beginning to crumble, for the panels of indestructible, purplish-dark flint. The flint had never been known to crumble or to make the least acknowledgement of multiplying aeons.

The guildhall stood in the small marketplace and was separated from Police H.Q. by three narrow streets. The marketplace was not now the centre of the town and had ceased to be so for one or two centuries. Its principal use was as a car park. It had only two small shops. In the middle of the morning it was usually deserted, and it was almost deserted when Gently parked there.

He locked his door, strolled over to the guildhall's spill of worn stone steps. A uniform man stood by the porch. He straightened, touched his helmet to Gently. Inside the building was cold and meagre, its gloom helped out by a few naked bulbs. Some grey cement stairs led up to a landing and to a varnished door labelled Court Room. Beside this stood a second uniform man. He was rocking ponderously on his heels.

'Your man isn't here yet, sir,' he told Gently. 'They're doing a bloke up for indecent exposure.'

'That should be edifying,' Gently said.

The man began to grin, thought better of it.

Gently went through the door. The courtroom was high-ceilinged and underlit. Its fixtures, sprouting over the whole floor space, were of brown wood and black iron. The dock on the left looked like a cattle-cage and the raked benches like pews. There were bad acoustics. The walls were grimy. The air was chill, damp, neglected.

He noticed Setters sitting on the right, staring boredly at the Counsels' tables, and near these, at another table, sat two reporters, also bored. In the public gallery sat Mrs Bixley, her eyes fixed mournfully on the Bench. She was one of only two spectators. The other one was Deeming.

Gently went into the gallery, seated himself beside Deeming. Deeming turned to give him a smile, then held up a finger.

'Listen a moment . . . this witness.'

He was leaning forward on the varnished partition. The voice of the witness was barely audible across the sound-deadening room. She was a dowdy, middle-aged woman in a rusty black coat. The tone of her voice was indignant and she held her chin tilted upwards.

'Magnificent!' Deeming whispered to Gently. 'Like she's the soul and bowels of Christ-ish hypocrisy. Man, the accused was a wild one when he piddled in front of her.'

'Was she what brought you here?' Gently asked.

'Like she's the bonus,' Deeming said. 'I've come to find out what you've got on Sidney. But keep it down, man, keep it down.'

He lowered his chin on the partition and continued to absorb the witness's testimony. Beyond him the bulk of Mrs Bixley shifted uneasily on the hard bench. She, too, was dressed in black, and she had artificial violets pinned to her lapel. She didn't pay any attention to Deeming, the Bench engaged her whole interest.

The case ended with a fine and some stiffish words from the magistrate. After some consultations, enterings, and exitings, a parking offence was heard.

'These are a drag,' Deeming said to Gently. 'Like thy ruin a morning at the court. If it wasn't for Sid coming on I'd duck out and leave it with them. What's Sid done – pitched a screw?'

Gently shrugged. 'You'll hear,' he said.

'I'm anxious about him,' Deeming said. 'I come here like a probation officer. Give me the action.'

'I think you know it,' Gently said.

'You mean like my pad being frisked?' Deeming asked. 'You were way off the beam there, screw. Nobody stashes their dope with me.'

'Somebody stashes it somewhere,' Gently said.

'Sure,' Deeming said. 'That stands to reason. But not in their own backyard they stash it. And not in my backyard, neither.'

'Where would you stash it?' Gently asked.

'Right under your nose,' Deeming grinned. 'Some place so obvious the screws wouldn't see it, like because they're seeing it every day. What do you say to the bridge near your hotel?'

'You'd need a boat,' Gently said.

'Yes,' Deeming said. 'That's a drawback, but I still think the bridge is good. Then there's the market cross outside here. You could stash some dope in the roof. Or maybe that sand-hopper outside the screw-shop. You had a look in your sand-hopper lately?'

'I'll make a point of it,' Gently said. 'Anywhere else you can think of?'

'Down in the forest,' Deeming said. 'Something might stir there.'

He grinned again, ran fingers through his short brown hair.

'Like stop fishing,' he said. 'I wouldn't help you if I could, screw. You make it a crime for these kids to get a touch out of smoking. That's Squaresville from Squaresville. It's no crime east of Suez.'

'I wouldn't know,' Gently said. 'It's outside our jurisdiction.'

Wit,' Deeming said, 'wit. I like your sense of humour, screw. Big deadpan stuff. I always go for it crazy. But it wasn't very bright to go hanging Sid up, not because he smokes a little. Sid's been keeping it pretty cool.'

'I'm glad to hear it,' Gently said.

'Yeah, pretty cool,' said Deeming. 'Considering what he used to be and all the action he's been through. You oughtn't to jump on a kid like that, you ought to lay on him light. Let him feel he's being something, don't sit on his ego. That way he'll cool some more. But if you push him, he'll keep flipping his lid. Man, even screws were young once, they ought to remember the way it is.'

'I can remember,' Gently said. 'Though I never stood in one of those.'

'Yeah, but you could have done,' Deeming said. 'That's the point, you could have done. You're fighting it out when you're a kid. You don't quite see the margins plain. You'll like as not step over the side and then you'll wonder why they're shouting. And all of a sudden you're getting shot at, you're a delinquent, you're branded. Like there isn't a couple of worlds between a criminal and his neighbour, and when you're young there's next to nothing. You could have stood there in that dock.'

'Say I was lucky.' Gently said.

Deeming caught him with a smile. 'Lucky it is,' he said. 'You take a point well, screw.'

'And Bixley's just misunderstood?' Gently said.

'Misunderstood,' Deeming said. 'Like you can give that "just" the air, it didn't sound very bright.'

'I was working late, this isn't my morning for being bright,' Gently said.

'Wit,' Deeming said. 'It sends me. Play Sid for a fine and let him loose.'

Setters came down the aisle for Gently. He didn't manage to see Deeming sitting there. Deeming grinned, gave a little bow. Setters kept not managing to see him.

'Bixley next,' he said to Gently. 'I've had a word with the Bench about it.'

Gently followed him back to the side-stall, took a seat beside Setters and Baynes.

Bixley was called and brought in from some subterranean region. He stalked defiantly into the cage and stood lounging against it. But there was a peakiness about him, he was continually jiffling, moving his hands. He looked sullenly about the court, he saw Deeming. Their eyes met. Mrs Bixley was standing up, but Bixley didn't look at her.

The preliminaries were gone through and Bixley represented. The Clerk of the Court addressed the magistrate. Gently was called. He gave sparse details of the charge, referring to the episode at Castlebridge; asked the Court for a remand in custody pending further investigation. Bixley's solicitor rose, made a formal objection. Gently answered it. The remand was granted. It all took exactly five minutes. And during that elapse of time Deeming hadn't taken his eyes off Bixley.

'So far, so good,' Setters said, as they went down the steps from the courtroom. 'Me, I'm still a bit surprised it's gone off so quietly. I thought we'd have seen his pals around, but no, only friend Dicky. What was he saying up there that pleased him so much?'

Gently shrugged. 'He was trying to sell me a line about Bixley.'

'It's his aim in life,' Setters said. 'He was selling me

some last night. I was praying I'd find that dope there all the time we were searching. I don't live clean, that's my trouble. But I'd love to see Dicky in the dock.'

He went with Baynes back to the Wolseley which had brought Bixley to the court. Gently returned to his Rover, prepared to follow the police car. When it came out of the side lane he could see Bixley in the back between Baynes and another detective constable. Gently fitted in behind it. They drove out of the square and into Tungate Street.

And in Tungate Street they saw the motorcycles, six, spread out and charging towards them.

From then on it went too fast to make a coherent picture.

Gently braked, nearly hit the Wolseley, and finished up with one wheel on the kerb. Other motorcycles were coming from behind them, they jam-packed the narrow street. Black-clad figures locked machines together and ran shouting towards the Wolseley. A brick crashed through one of its windows. A door was pulled open, a man dragged out. Setters, a flailing fury, came jack-in-a-boxing into the fight. Baynes was struggling in the back with Bixley, he was trying to get some cuffs on to him. Gently launched out of the Rover. He downed a couple of assailants who set on him. As he got to the Wolseley he heard a cry from Baynes and saw Bixley come out holding a bloodied flick-knife. He saw Gently. He came at him. His mouth was dragged down at one corner. His eyes were flinching and small, the brows knotted, twitching. He didn't say anything. He came at Gently.

He held the blade pointing at Gently's stomach. He lunged. Gently struck down the blade. Then he nearly decapitated Bixley with the side of his hand.

Bixley folded with a choking shriek and the knife went shimmying along the tarmac. Gently kicked it under the car, began hauling attackers from the man who was down. Baynes staggered out of the car, his arm bloody, stood with his back to the car and kicked. Setters was chopping away near the bonnet. He was shouting something about the radio. The man down got to his feet. There were several attackers on the floor. Suddenly, it seemed, the fighting wavered, the shouting stopped, there was a hush. The black-leathered gang drew off in a group, stood panting together, staring at the policemen. They saw the blood rippling down Baynes's arm. They saw Bixley writhing and choking. They looked surprised and at a loss, couldn't determine what to do.

'Yuh, get Sid,' one of them said. The voice sounded like Hallman's. All of them were wearing black stocking-masks with leather helmets and goggles. 'Yuh, get Sid and let's get out of here.' But a curious paralysis seemed to have come over them. They kept panting, standing close, some of them crouching as though expecting an attack. Gently picked up Bixley, slung him into the back of the car. Nobody moved to prevent him. They merely watched with rounded eyes. He went to the nearest pair of motorcycles, ripped the leads from the plugs. Still they watched him, motionless. And they watched Baynes's arm.

Then Baynes collapsed. He did it so quietly that it looked like a slow-motion film shot. He swayed forward a little, then his knees went, then he flopped lazily to the street. It acted as a trigger. There was a commotion. They rushed in a panic for the bikes. Setters burst at them with a roar, kicking down bikes and clumping heads. In a moment they were fighting again, but now it was a disorganized, divided fighting, with the attackers on the run and trying to get their bikes started. At the same time reinforcements arrived. A patrol car came squealing in from the square. From the other direction a whistle was sounding, a uniform man pounded earnestly up the street.

'Stop them – stop them!' Setters was bawling. 'Use force – don't let them go!'

One of them had got a motorcycle going but he swerved round the constable and came off. Others were abandoning their machines, they were trying to dodge away up a side-turn. Four uniform men jumped out of the patrol car, came running in an extended line. One of the fugitives tried to break through it and was felled for his pains. Setters commanded the side-turn, Gently and the other two completed the cordon. They'd trapped eight of them out of twelve, and all the bikes had been left behind. Eight scared, gasping, gang-boys, three of them down on the ground. They huddled together sheep-like. Blood was showing through some of their masks.

'Right!' Setters panted. 'We'll have them handcuffed in pairs. Simpson, you see to Baynes, the poor swine has been knifed.'

The cordon closed in. It shouldered the fugitives into a tight circle. Hallman ducked and started to bolt for it, but Gently's hand settled on his collar. He was hoiked back whimpering, the cold steel snapped on his wrist. The others didn't give any trouble. One of them could scarcely stand.

In the back of the Wolseley Bixley still lay gagging and groaning.

Beside the Wolseley Simpson was slitting Baynes's sleeve to reveal an ugly, gashed wound.

Setters hissed. He was trembling.

'Christ,' he muttered, 'that chummie's lucky. I'd have hit him, I would. I'd have bloody well killed him.'

'Keep an eye on my car,' Gently said. 'There's a call I want to pay.'

'I'd have killed him,' Setters muttered. 'I'd have beat his brains out on the kerb.'

Gently hurried back up Tungate Street, across the market square to the guildhall. The uniform man on the door was kicking his heels, but he clicked them together when he saw Gently.

'Has Deeming left?' Gently demanded.

'Deeming . . . ? No, sir,' the man said.

Gently hurried on up.

In the courtroom they were fining a housewife for having a defective rear light on her bicycle. Mrs Bixley had left the public gallery, Deeming was sitting there alone. He turned to give Gently a grin.

'Come out here,' Gently said to him.

'Like that's an order?' Deeming grinned.

'It's an order,' Gently said.

Deeming rose, stretching himself leisurely. 'It's getting tame, anyway,' he said. 'Sid and the gent who was indecent were like the star turns this morning.'

'Come out here on the landing.'

'Sure, sure,' Deeming said. 'I always like to oblige a screw. But you're sweating, man. What's the action?'

The courtroom door closed behind them. Gently shepherded Deeming along to the end of the landing. He stood him under one of the bulbs, gave him a long, silent look.

'Mysteriouser,' Deeming grinned, 'and mysteriouser, this gets. What's all the steam and puff about? Like perhaps you thought I wouldn't be here?'

'We've still got Sid,' Gently said.

'Congratulations,' Deeming said.

'And eight of the others,' Gently said. 'And all twelve of their bikes.'

'I'll catch on,' Deeming said. 'Don't tell me, just keep on talking.'

'Sid had a knife,' Gently said. 'He put it into one of Setters's men.'

The grin went off Deeming's face. 'I don't like that bit,' he said. 'Where would Sid get a blade from?'

'I'd like to know,' Gently said.

Deeming's face was right blank. 'Jeebies don't use blades,' he said.

'Sid had a blade,' Gently said.

'Yeah,' Deeming said. 'You keep giving it to me. But where did he get it from, then – like you searched him when he was pinched?'

'He was searched,' Gently said. 'He didn't have a blade then.'

Deeming's slate eyes smiled. 'So,' he said, 'what's the

curve? You think I slipped Sid a knife from up in the gallery this morning?'

'I think he was slipped a knife,' Gently said. 'And I think I know when it was slipped. And I've been asking myself why – what was the reason for slipping him a knife?'

'Like to give him a weapon,' Deeming said.

'Yes,' Gently said. 'To give him a weapon. And right at the psychological moment when he might be tempted to use it.'

'You think that?' Deeming asked.

Gently nodded. 'I think that. So he might have killed a man. So he might have been going to swing anyway.'

'Subtle,' Deeming said.

'Yes,' Gently said, 'subtle.'

'Like someone had got it in for Sid,' Deeming said.

'Just like that,' Gently said.

'And you know why?' Deeming said. 'Don't be a square and leave me hanging.'

'I thought you could give me the reason,' Gently said. 'Why someone should make us a present of Sid.'

Deeming chuckled. 'You're a crazy screw. I get a wild kick out of you, man. Like what should I know about this action, sitting up here and minding my business? Like when did Sid start carving up the screws?'

'And that's your answer?' Gently said.

'Yuh,' Deeming said. 'That's about my answer. I don't go for mixing in screw-fights, screw.'

'We've taken them in,' Gently said. 'There'll be twelve interrogations.'

'Sounds like work,' Deeming said. 'I hope it's worth what you put into it.'

'Then there's Bixley,' Gently said. 'He hasn't smoked for fourteen hours.'

'Tough,' Deeming said, 'tough. Like I hope you're treating him right otherwise.'

'He could talk,' Gently said.

'Yuh,' Deeming said, 'Sid can talk. Maybe not now so's a jury could believe him, but you can't expect it, after carving screws. Leaves a bad taste in people's mouths. Like they think you're maybe lying your head off.'

'Still, we can listen,' Gently said.

'It's what screws are for,' Deeming said. 'And its sad, all this about Sid. I'm really grieved, in my way.'

He slid up his sleeve, looked at his watch, dropped his hand again.

'You finished with me, screw,' he said, 'or like you're going to sound off some more?'

'I haven't finished with you,' Gently said. 'But you can get to hell out of it.'

'Subtle,' Deeming said. 'I take a hint. You're too suspicious screw. By half.'

He lounged away, down the stairs, gave the man on the door a cheery good morning. Gently spent a second staring after him, then he whisked along to the courtroom again.

'Where's the phone?' he demanded.

'In the office, sir,' the constable told him.

He showed Gently into an icy room which had a roll-top desk and an old safe in it. On the back of the desk stood an upright instrument. Gently unhooked it and asked for Police H.Q.

'Has Inspector Setters got back yet?'

'Yes, sir . . . he's just come in.'

'Put him on.'

In a couple of moments Setters snarled 'Yeah?' into his instrument.

Gently said: 'I want a couple of men with a car to tail Deeming. He's just now left the guildhall and is probably walking back to his rooms. They needn't be clever about tailing him, in fact I'd like him to know they're there, but they've got to stick with him, on or off his bike, and keep in R.T. contact with H.Q. If he gets away from them on his bike they're to alert the patrols to intercept him. And it's urgent. I want your men to pick him up right away.'

Setters hesitated. 'For how long,' he asked, 'am I losing these two men and a car?'

'Not very long,' Gently replied. 'Not very long is the way I see it.'

CHAPTER ELEVEN

DURING THE WHOLE of the incident in Tungate Street the street had been completely deserted, but now, when Gently went back for his car, the place was crowded with sightseers. The bikes had not yet been taken away and were being guarded by two uniform men, and on the spot where Baynes had lain bleeding some sawdust had been hastily strewn. The two reporters from the courtroom had got there and had been joined by a photographer. His flashbulb hissed as Gently came up and the two reporters jumped in eagerly.

'Can you give us a statement, Superintendent?'

'Try Inspector Setters,' Gently said.

'But this is your car – you were here when it happened?'

'No comment,' Gently said.

'What was the name of the wounded man?'

'No comment,' Gently said.

'Is it true that this connects with the Lister case?'

'I'll give you a statement later,' Gently said.

'Then we can assume there is a connection?'

'No comment,' Gently said.

He pushed them aside, got in his car, backed off the kerb, and drove away. The crowd parted to let him through, each one peering to get a glimpse of him. At Police H.Q. there was another crowd, more reporters and photographers. He shouldered through them, head down, deaf to the fresh questions flung at him.

Setters was sitting alone in his office, his face pale, trembling still. He didn't look up when Gently came in. His hand was resting on his telephone.

'They've got him up in the hospital,' he said. 'Simpson is with him. They're giving him a transfusion. It just happens he's one of those types that keep on bleeding. It could be fatal to him. Simpson's in the same group.'

'That's the way things happen,' Gently said.

Setters looked at him. His eyes were glittering.

'You didn't hit that bloody slob hard enough,' he said. 'He's spewing his guts up in the cell. Christ, if he'd come at me with a knife!'

Gently gave him a slow nod.

'I'm not responsible,' Setters said. 'When a slob like that cuts loose with a knife I don't want law. I stop being a cop.'

'Did you pick up the knife?' Gently asked.

Setters pointed to a scrap of paper on the desk. Folded in it was the bloodied flick-knife with some dirt and fluff stuck to the blade. It was a common pattern and appeared to be new. It had a fibre handle with diamond embossings.

'Could that have been bought locally?' Gently asked.

Setters shrugged faintly. 'I'll check it,' he said. 'I could bloody weep. I'm no good as a cop. I think for sure I'd have killed that slob.'

'You wouldn't have killed him,' Gently said.

'Look at me,' Setters said. 'Look at the way I'm shaking. I'm a Detective Inspector, me, I've got thirty years' service. And I'm just finding out I've got murder in me.'

'Not murder,' Gently said. 'Blind hate, that's all.'

'Murder,' Setters said. 'Murder. I know what I feel. When I saw him go for you with that knife I wanted to smash the life out of him. I wanted to do it then and there. And I'd have done it, I'm bloody certain.'

Gently shook his head. 'You wouldn't be talking about it now,' he said. 'The ones who'll do it don't talk about it. They only talk with their hands.'

Setters looked at his hands. He moved the fingers, crooking them.

'I could bloody weep,' he repeated. He jammed his hands into his pockets.

Gently sat on the desk, filled his pipe, gave one or two puffs.

'Did you notice who slipped Bixley the knife?' he asked.

'Nope,' Setters said. 'I was bawling into the R.T. It must have been after they pulled out Brewer, after the window was smashed.'

'Brewer didn't see it?'

'Didn't have a chance,' Setters said. 'Baynes must have seen it slipped, but we can't talk to him. How would he have recognized him, anyway, when the slob had a mask?'

'He might have said something,' Gently said. 'Baynes might have recognized the voice.'

'Yes,' Setters said. 'There's a chance of that. And we'll get whoever it was if I have to use a rack on them. I want that chummie in the dock along with Bixley.'

'There'll be no prints on that handle,' Gently said. 'But we might be able to trace the purchase.'

Setters gave the knife a glare. 'I don't think it was bought here,' he said. 'There's only two shops would sell them, and I keep an eye on what they stock. It's ten years since we had any knife business in Latchford. Maybe you can buy them in Castlebridge.'

'You can buy them in Bethnal,' Gently said.

'Yes,' Setters said, 'that sounds more likely. But I'll check, don't worry. I want every screw in Bixley's coffin. And I'm telling you this, too. I've forgotten that Elton ever existed. Just nail that Lister job on Bixley, and Elton can go chase his tail.'

Gently smiled distantly, puffing. 'I may oblige with that,' he said.

'He's the chummie,' Setters said. 'I can see it now, the murdering slob. Elton was just a mixed-up kid, he didn't have it in him to kill. But Bixley's a killer, a filthy killer. He did that job, and he's going to swing.'

'Yes,' Gently said, 'it was subtle.'

'Subtle my foot,' Setters snarled. 'Just subtle him along to the eight o'clock walk, that's subtle enough for a thug like him.'

The phone belted. Setters snatched it.

'It's for you,' he said. 'I'm crossing my fingers.'

It was Pagram on the other end, he was sounding smooth and allusive. Gently moved his pipe across and kept puffing while he listened.

'Yes,' he said at last. 'Thank you. My congratulations to Narcotics.' He paused some puffs. 'No,' he said. 'Just send the report up by dispatch.'

He hung up. 'That's it,' he said. 'Another screw for Bixley's coffin. His cousin came clean after an all-night session, and we've chapter and verse for the dope-peddling charge.'

'Fine,' Setters said. 'But it's not enough, now.'

'Mmn,' Gently nodded. 'It's the link we wanted. It was only surmise up till now, but now the surmise is proved. We've got a motive for the Lister killing. Lister was interfering with the trade.'

'They won't hang him on the motive,' Setters said.

'No,' Gently said, 'but we've got our link.' He went on smoking, looking at the knife. 'We've got to clinch it now,' he said.

'So?' Setters said.

Gently rose from the desk. 'I'll back a hunch,' he said. 'Have them send in Hallman for a little chat. I'm guessing he knows as much as anybody.'

Hallman was sent in. He wasn't looking very happy. He'd got a bruise on his cheek and a strip of plaster on his chin. He'd got plaster on his hand as well, across the lower palm of his left hand. He was trying to stare at people defiantly. He wasn't managing it too well.

'Sit down, Hallman,' Gently said, pointing to the

chair they'd placed for him. This time the chair was close to the desk and only the light from the window fell on it. Setters had kept sitting behind the desk. Gently had resumed his perch on it. He had refilled his pipe and was now lighting it, talking with his pipe in his mouth.

Hallman sat, clasping his hands between his legs. Gently put out his match, puffed, looked at Hallman.

'You've hurt your hand,' Gently said to him.

Hallman clasped it a bit tighter.

'Is it badly cut?' Gently said.

Hallman didn't give an answer.

Gently went on surveying him mildly, giving regular, thoughtful, puffs. He clasped his hands round one knee, leaning a little closer to Hallman.

'You're in a bit of trouble, Hallman,' he said. 'I think you're going to get sent to jail. We know quite a lot about you and Bixley, more than you're giving us credit for. You know what I'm talking about, Hallman?'

Hallman kneaded his clasped hands.

'Yes,' Gently said. 'You're in pretty deep. So it's no use your hiding that hand up.'

'I ain't hiding it up,' Hallman said, but without displaying his hand.

'How did you cut it?' Gently asked.

'It ain't cut,' Hallman said.

Gently stuck out his hand. 'Show it to me,' he said.

'It ain't cut,' Hallman persisted. 'Like I tore it on something.'

'On what?'

Hallman pulled on his hands, writhed his shoulders from side to side.

'On my handlebars,' he said. 'Yuh, on my handlebars, that's what.'

'You've got something sharp on your handlebars?'

'Yuh, something,' Hallman said. 'Like I threw my bike down quick and cotched my hand on something.'

'Are you left-handed?' Gently asked.

'No,' Hallman said. 'Right-handed, I am.'

'So you threw your bike down to your right – yet you tore your left hand.'

'Yuh,' Hallman said. 'Yuh, that's how I did it. Yuh.'

'You're a poor liar,' Gently said.

'Yuh, it ain't a lie,' Hallman said.

Gently puffed smoke over his head. 'Remember I was there,' he said. 'I was watching you, Hallman. I saw every move you made. It was you who smashed the window with a brick. It was the rear window on the car's right. Then you had to reach in and forward to unlock it, and you used your left hand to do that. You've got a clean cut on your palm, Hallman. You cut it on the jagged edge of the window.'

'No, I never,' Hallman said. 'Like on my handlebars I did it. Nor I didn't throw no brick, you didn't see me do that.'

'Perhaps you weren't there?' Gently said.

'Yuh,' Hallman said, 'I was there.'

'You're sure of that?' Gently said.

'Yuh,' Hallman said. 'Yuh.'

Gently flipped open the paper on the desk, revealed the knife with its blood and dirt. He just held his finger on the paper for a moment, watching Hallman stare at the knife.

'What would that be?' Gently asked.

Hallman swallowed. 'That's a blade,' he said.

'What blade would it be?' Gently asked.

'Yuh, I don't know,' Hallman said.

'You don't know?' Gently asked.

'I ain't never seen it,' Hallman said. 'Yuh, never seen it I haven't. I don't know nothing about that.'

'You aren't trying,' Gently said.

'It's true what I'm saying,' Hallman said. 'I ain't never had a blade, nor I don't know nothing about that one.'

'Somebody got hurt,' Gently said. 'You know about that, don't you, Hallman? He's in the hospital, Hallman. He's having a blood transfusion. And he may not recover from it, Hallman. That knife there may have killed him. So that will make it murder, Hallman. That will make it capital murder.'

'I tell you I ain't never seen that blade – I didn't do it!' Hallman yelped.

'But you know who did do it,' Gently said. 'Who was it stuck this knife into Baynes?'

'I never saw that!'

'Yes, you did,' Gently said. 'You were right on the spot when it happened.'

'Sid,' Hallman said, 'he was sitting next to Baynes.'

Gently nodded. 'But where did Sid get the knife from?' he asked.

Hallman twisted about on the chair. 'How should I know?' he said. 'I didn't have no part in that – it's the truth, I never!'

'Who gave you that knife?' Gently asked.

'Nobody didn't give it to me.'

'Who gave you that knife?' Gently asked.

'I ain't never seen it. I ain't. I ain't!'

'You're in trouble,' Gently said. 'You're in very grave trouble. You'd better start thinking about getting out from under it, Hallman. Lying isn't going to help you, we know too much about it for that. Only giving us cooperation is going to help you now. So I'm asking you again – who gave you that knife?'

'Nobody didn't, I tell you – not nobody!' Hallman screamed.

'Who planned this business?'

'Nobody. Nobody planned it.'

'It planned itself?'

'We got together, we just got together!' Hallman wailed.

'You just got together, and nobody planned it. Nobody said it would be a wild kick. Nobody pinpointed Tungate Street, or suggested that Sid should be slipped a blade.'

'Yuh, nobody, nobody!' Hallman gulped. 'Just to give him a break, that's all it was. There wasn't no blades, no nothing about it. Not nobody didn't give me that blade.'

'So where did it come from?' Gently asked.

'I don't know where it come from. I ain't never seen it.'

'Who opened the door and slipped it to Bixley?'

'I wasn't never near the door,' Hallman wailed.

'You weren't made for a liar,' Gently said. He let the paper fold back over the knife. Still Hallman couldn't take his eyes from it, they stared at the paper, distended, unseeing. Gently put a fresh match to his pipe, broke up the match, dropped it in the tray. He directed a stream of smoke at Hallman.

'What do you know about Lister?' he asked.

Hallman jerked. His eyes jumped from the paper.

'Nothing about him I don't know,' he said.

Gently made a clicking sound with his tongue. 'Not anything at all about Lister?' he asked.

'Yuh, like I saw him around,' Hallman said. 'That's all it was. I saw him around.'

'You saw him around,' Gently said. 'You saw a great deal of Lister. Maybe you saw him on Tuesday night. Did you see him on Tuesday night, Hallman?'

'No,' Hallman said. 'I never. I was at home. I didn't see him.'

'Nor any time on the Tuesday?'

'Not any time Tuesday,' Hallman said.

'Lister,' Gently said, 'didn't like Bixley, did he?'

'Yuh,' Hallman said. 'He liked him.'

'I don't think he did,' Gently said.

'Yuh, so what if he didn't?' Hallman said.

'Why didn't he like him?' Gently asked.

'He just didn't like him,' Hallman said.

'Because of the reefers?' Gently asked.

'Yuh,' Hallman said. 'It might have been that.'

'Why because of that?' Gently asked.

'I don't know,' Hallman said.

'You'd better know something,' Gently said. 'In case we find your prints on this knife.'

Hallman flinched, dragged on his hands. 'Yuh,' he said. 'It could have been the girl.'

'Betty Turner?' Gently asked.

'Yuh, Betty Turner,' Hallman said.

'You're telling me that Bixley was jealous about her?'

'Yuh,' Hallman said. 'Could be.'

Gently sighed, picked up the knife. 'We'd better get this to prints,' he said.

Setters nodded. 'I'm tired of his lies. He can tell the rest of them to the jury.'

'Listen!' Hallman blabbered. 'Listen. I can tell you why Lister had it in for him. Lister didn't go for it, not smoking sticks. It's the truth what I'm telling you.'

'We found reefers at his home,' Gently said.

'Yuh, he didn't go for it,' Hallman said. 'You ask them. Ask any of them. They all know he didn't go for it. That's why he had it in for Sid, it's the truth, it is. He found out Sid was pushing the sticks, he got his knife into Sid.'

'He found out that Bixley was supplying the reefers?'

'Yuh, it's the truth,' Hallman whined. 'He flipped his lid. He was mad about it. You ask any of the jees.'

'Why,' Gently said, 'did he flip his lid?'

'It's like I'm telling you!' Hallman said. 'Sid was pushing the stuff to Lister's chick and Lister rumbled he was doing it.'

'Because he was selling reefers to Betty Turner?'

'Yuh, yuh,' Hallman said. 'And he flipped his lid one night at Tony's, said he was going to stop Sid pushing them.'

'Well, well,' Gently said.

'I'm telling you straight,' Hallman wailed. 'Ask Tony, ask anyone. They all know about that.'

'What else do they know,' Gently said. 'What else do you know, Hallman? Did Sid tell his pals what happened on Tuesday, or did he just keep ever so quiet?'

'He didn't say nothing about Tuesday,' Hallman said.

'He was being modest,' Gently said.

'Not nothing to nobody,' Hallman said.

'Over-modest,' said Gently.

He sat slowly breathing out smoke, looking through and beyond Hallman. Hallman went on kneading his hands as though he wanted to make dough of them. Gently absently poked the knife.

'Where does Bixley keep them?' he asked.

Hallman jerked. 'Like what?' he said.

'His hoard of reefers,' Gently said. 'You're in the know with Sid, aren't you?'

'No,' Hallman said. 'He ain't told no one about them.'

'Would Elton have known?' Gently asked.

'I don't know about him,' Hallman whined.

Gently nodded. 'Right,' he said. 'You can go back to do some thinking, Hallman. You'll have plenty to think about I expect. Perhaps we can talk again later.'

'That ain't my knife,' Hallman said.

'Think about it,' Gently said.

'Yuh,' Hallman said. 'It's the truth I've been telling you.'

He was taken out.

Setters edged for the telephone, took his hand away again; lit a cigarette instead and blasted smoke down his nose.

'Can we prove it on him?' he asked. 'That he was the slob who gave Bixley the knife?'

Gently shrugged. 'With a bit of luck. That knife had to get to Bixley somehow.'

'Yeah,' Setters said. 'And I like that cut hand. You figured that out very nicely. I'm going to tie that up right tight, I'm going to have two medics report on it. Nobody's getting out of this case. It's going in like a block of concrete.'

He got out of his chair, walked up and down.

'You've got a rhythm,' he said. 'You did a beautiful job on that punk, you squeezed him for just what you wanted. A little more, and we've fixed Bixley. I want him topped, not put away.'

'It's still circumstantial,' Gently said. 'And that alibi might beat us. Elton's the king-pin of the case. Find Elton, and we're home.'

Setters stopped, his back to Gently.

'You think we're going to find him?' he said.

'I don't know,' Gently shrugged at nobody. 'I wouldn't be Elton,' he said, 'at the moment.'

'Bixley can't get at him,' Setters said.

'No,' Gently said. 'Not Bixley.'

Setters came round. 'Dicky?' he asked.

Gently nodded his slow nod.

'Yeah,' Setters said. 'Dicky. I'm the dumb cluck, aren't I? I didn't quite get through to that one, even when you had me put a tail on him. Dicky. Little Dicky Deeming. The lad who likes to play his records. The boy who gave us this jeebie stuff. Deeming. Little Dicky Deeming.' He paused, sucked some smoke. 'And you think he'll lead us to Elton?' he asked.

'If Elton's alive,' Gently said. 'Which I'm afraid doesn't follow.'

'But if he is,' Setters persisted, 'you reckon Deeming will pay him a visit? Deeming's in the know about Elton, he knows that Elton's evidence will fix Bixley. So he pays Elton a visit to try to make sure that he won't come out till after the trial. You reckon he can put some pressure on Elton – maybe shift him to another place?'

'He can kill him,' Gently said.

'Kill him?' Setters stared hard. 'He can't be that much in love with Bixley, not to go round killing people.'

'He's in love with himself,' Gently said. 'That's the way it is with killers. And he'll kill Elton if he gets to him. Elton's life isn't worth a pin.'

Setters was quiet for a moment. Then he said: 'Are you trying to tell me something?'

Gently gave him his nod again. 'Deeming killed Lister,' he said.

Setters was quiet again. He punched the smoke through his nostrils. He came back to his chair, sat down on it, leaned his elbows, stared at nothing.

'It hurts,' he said at last. 'I'm trying to go with you, but it hurts. I've got no class as a policeman. I just want Bixley topped.'

'You took Deeming's alibi,' Gently said.

'Yes,' Setters said. 'I can remember. He was up at Tony's till five to midnight. Tony said so. The others said so.'

'It isn't a good one,' Gently said. 'And nobody asked Tony if a call came for Deeming.'

'But it could have done,' Setters said. 'Bixley could have rung Deeming at Tony's.'

Gently went on nodding. 'He'd have rung him,' he said. 'Deeming was the brain in the Bixley set-up. Bixley would have rung him when he was in trouble. And he was in trouble last Tuesday night. Lister had found out where Bixley was collecting the reefers, and Lister had sworn to put a stop to it. He was going to blow the whistle on Bixley. Bixley rang Deeming and told him what had happened.'

'And Deeming laid for Lister,' Setters said.

'Yes,' Gently said. 'There was no other way. Lister was angry, he couldn't be talked out of it, he'd have busted the racket wide open. But he was vulnerable, he was on the road, he was where Deeming could deal with him. There could be a crash that would look quite natural, and no awkward questions afterwards. It was Elton who complicated the job. He was tagging along behind Lister and Betty Turner. So he saw what happened, he knew who did it, he was in a spot from the beginning.'

'He was a smoker,' Setters said. 'They could put some pressure on him.'

'Yes,' Gently said. 'While he was loose. But it worked against them if he was held. It was touch and go for them when you weren't satisfied and started making a play for Elton. If he'd been kept away from his dope he would probably have cracked and told the truth. So Elton had to disappear, and he went as soon as they could get at him. I like to think he's still alive, but I can't think of any reason for it.'

'I ought to have held him,' Setters said. 'The murdering slobs. I gave them the chance.'

Gently shook his head. 'You did the right thing. You weren't certain, so you didn't charge.'

'It'll be on my conscience,' Setters said. He crammed his cigarette butt into the tray. 'If he's dead,' he muttered to himself. He took his hands off the desk.

'We've got the same theme recurring with Bixley,' Gently said. 'He's a smoker, and we're holding him, and there's a danger he might crack. I don't think he will, but the danger's there, and Deeming could see that danger. That's why Bixley found a knife in his hand when the ambush was pulled.'

'It's coming to me,' Setters said. 'That's what you were driving at just now. Hallman didn't just happen to have a knife by him which he handed to Bixley.'

'There was no object in it,' Gently said. 'Hallman wouldn't have thought of a knife. You say yourself there's been no knife trouble in Latchford lately.'

'Deeming wanted Bixley to buy something.'

'Yes,' Gently said. 'The lot. Then we wouldn't pay any attention to what he might tell us about Deeming and Lister. Coming after Bixley had knifed a policeman, it wouldn't sound very convincing. The more he told it, the more we'd think he did the Lister job himself. And no Elton, no proof. We couldn't do a thing to Dicky. Hallman's too much concerned with his hide to admit any knowledge of the knife.'

'And I was falling for that,' Setters said, pressing his arms against the desk. 'I was falling right into it. It'd have gone the way you said. All I could see was chummie Bixley with that knife in his hand. I can't see much more now. It's one of those things that stick.'

Gently nodded. 'Bixley was a tool. It doesn't excuse him, but he was one. Deeming was throwing him to the wolves, there can be no doubt about that. And we haven't proved it yet, Deeming's still riding high. And Bixley can't prove it for us. He can only tell us where to look for Elton.'

'He's going to tell us,' Setters said.

Gently shrugged. 'It won't be easy. Bixley's tough. He'll never accept Deeming's treachery on our say-so.'

'He'll tell us,' Setters said.

'Also, he's implicated,' Gently said.

'Sooner or later,' Setters said, 'he's going to tell us but everything.'

The door was tapped, Simpson entered. Setters came up off his chair.

'It's all right,' Simpson said. 'He's all right. They've fixed him up. They had to do an artery job and stitch him, I can't remember what they called it. But he's all right, just weak. He had a pint or more from me.'

Setters slowly sat again. 'Thanks, Simpson,' he said. 'Thanks a lot. You'd better knock off. You can come in in the morning if you feel fit.'

'I'm fine,' Simpson said. 'A pint of blood doesn't worry me. And I've brought a message from the medics. You can talk to Betty Turner.'

'How's that?' Setters said.

'Betty Turner,' Simpson said. 'She's on the mend, she came round last night. You can talk to her if you want to.'

CHAPTER TWELVE

THE HOSPITAL AT Latchford was the South West Northshire and it stood on a swell of rising ground to the north of the town. It had a Georgian foundation which had been added to at other periods, the last addition being a modern ward block connected to two new theatres. Betty Turner was in the modern block, which was the furthest from the car park. After entering the spacious main hall they had to trek down several corridors. A lift took them to the second floor where they were met by the ward sister. She was a determined, strong-voiced woman who read them a lecture as she led them to the room.

'Five minutes only, and the patient is not to be worried. She is still quite weak and I will not allow her to be hectored.'

'Does she know we're coming?' Gently asked.

'Of course,' the ward sister replied. 'She asked to be permitted to see you. That's why you are here.'

She took them into a small room with a large window overlooking the town. By the window stood a white-painted bed in which a girl lay propped up with pillows. She had a snub nose and a rounded chin and her head was capped with a bandage. She looked towards the door eagerly. The ward sister closed the door and stood by it.

'Miss Turner?' Gently said.

'Yes,' the girl said. 'I'm Betty Turner.'

'I'm Superintendent Gently,' Gently said. 'I'm glad to hear you're getting better.'

'Are you a policeman?' Betty said.

'Yes,' Gently said. 'They tell me so.'

'I know *he's* a policeman,' Betty said. 'But I don't think I've seen you before.'

'The super's from the Yard,' Setters said. 'He knows all about the accident, Betty.'

She blushed underneath her bandage. 'Oh,' she said. 'I didn't know.'

Gently sat on the chair near the bed, spread himself, put his hat on his knees.

'You wanted to see us, Miss Turner,' he said. 'Have you remembered something else about the accident?'

She nodded, still looking doubtful. 'Has there been much . . . much fuss about it?' she asked.

'A little fuss,' Gently said. 'There always fuss in these cases.'

'I didn't know,' she repeated. She moved her hand under the quilt. 'I just wanted to tell you,' she said suddenly, 'that it couldn't have been Laurie who bumped into us.'

'Laurie Elton?' Gently asked.

'Yes,' she said. 'It couldn't have been Laurie. I knew

there was a reason why it couldn't be, but I haven't been able to think. He was going too fast, that's why.'

'Who was going too fast?' Gently asked.

'The man. The one who bumped into us. He was going a lot faster than we were, and Johnnie was flat out just there.'

'So it couldn't have been Elton catching you up?'

'No,' Betty said. 'It just couldn't have been. Laurie's bike is an old Ariel, it couldn't make the ton anyway. He was behind us all the way . . . he wasn't very pleased with me. We could see his lights miles away. The man who bumped us came from nowhere.'

'How do you mean – came from nowhere?'

'Well, we never saw him,' Betty said. 'You can see an awful long way there, and there was nobody behind us except Laurie. Then all of a sudden there was this other light catching us up like mad . . . and then . . . and then . . .' A shiver went through her. 'I knew,' she said. 'I knew he would hit us.'

The ward sister cleared her throat. Betty laid her head back on the pillows. She had a small, pretty mouth and the mouth was trembling.

'So that's how I know,' she said. 'Poor old Laurie wouldn't have done it.'

'Mmn,' Gently said. 'That takes care of that point, Miss Turner.'

'Poor Laurie,' she said. 'I wasn't very nice to Laurie.'

'Yes,' Gently said. 'But now I'd like to go back to that jazz session, Miss Turner.'

Her eyes darted to him, held there. 'I don't remember much about it,' she said.

'I don't want you to remember much,' Gently said. 'Just what happened about the box of chocolates.'

'Oh those.' She dropped her eyes. 'It wasn't anything, really,' she said. 'Sid Bixley won a box of chocolates. Johnny took them, for a lark.'

'For a lark?' Gently said.

'Yes,' she said. 'He didn't mean anything, honestly. He just picked them up as we were leaving. I'm sure he meant to give them back.'

Gently picked up his hat, made a fanning motion with it. He stared out of the window.

'It won't do,' he said, 'Miss Turner. You'll have to remember a little more.'

She blushed more deeply. 'It wasn't anything to do with me,' she said.

'I think it was,' Gently said. 'But you needn't tell me about that. Just why Johnny took that box of chocolates, and what he intended doing with them.'

She moved around under the quilt, took a great interest in the sheet turn-down. The ward sister was rumbling a little, shifted, made a noise with her keys.

'I could add,' Gently said, 'that there'll be no more jazz sessions at the Ten Spot. And that Sidney Bixley is in custody, charged with trading in reefers and other matters.'

'Oh,' she said. 'I see.' She continued staring at the turn-down. Well,' she said. 'You know all about it. There doesn't seem much for me to tell you.'

'It's just routine,' Gently urged. 'We like to get the details straight.'

She nodded her bandages. 'I suppose so,' she said. 'In

that case I'd better tell you. He – Johnny – didn't like me doing it . . . you know. Smoking those things. I was silly. Sid gave me a couple, just to try them, he said. Then I wanted some more, and he sold me some, and after that I kept buying them. And Johnny found out. He thought it was because of them that I . . . well, cooled off him a bit.'

'Was it because of that?' Gently asked.

'Oh no,' she said, 'it had nothing to do with it. I liked Johnny an awful lot, but he kept wanting us to get married, you know. But he thought it was the reefers, it was no good me saying anything. Then once he caught Sid selling me some. He got ever so angry about Sid.'

'When was that – on Tuesday morning?'

'Yes,' she said. 'You know about it? Johnny took the reefers away from me, lucky I'd got a couple to go on with.'

'In the Kummin Kafe,' Gently said.

'Yes.' She nodded. 'You know it all, don't you? And Johnny talked to me like a Dutch Uncle – he's an awfully serious boy, Johnny is. How is he getting on, please?'

A little explosion came from the ward sister.

'He's comfortable,' Gently said. 'You don't need to worry about Johnny.'

'I'm glad,' Betty said. 'They wouldn't tell me anything about him. And I do like Johnny, even though I wasn't, you know, in love with him.'

'Go on about Tuesday night,' Gently said.

'Yes,' she said. 'Well, Johnny was upset. He didn't say

anything more about the reefers, but he was awfully quiet and sort of offhand. He kept watching Sid and Ann Wicks when we were in the Ten Spot, and when Sid got the chocolates he seemed to get all excited. Then he said we were going to leave early, as soon as they'd played the last number, and as we went out he just picked up the chocolates – Sid had given them to Ann, she'd put them with her bag.'

'Did Bixley see Johnny take them?'

'No – he couldn't have done, could he? Anyway, he didn't come after us. I'm sure nobody noticed.'

'Did you meet anyone as you went through the milk bar?' Gently asked.

She shook her head. 'They were all down below. There was only that blonde woman who serves there.'

'Did she speak to you?'

'No,' Betty said. 'Just stared at us, that's all.'

'Mmn.' Gently nodded. 'So what happened when you got outside?'

'Well,' Betty said, 'Johnny opened the chocolates and found the reefers underneath. Laurie came out just then, so Johnny stuck them in his saddlebag. Then he started up and we got away, and Laurie followed behind.'

'Did Johnny say what he was going to do?'

'He said he was going to the police when he got back. I was awfully scared about it all. But he said he wouldn't mention me.'

'And that's all . . . till Five Mile Drove?'

The bandages nodded. 'Yes. That's all.'

'Thank you, Miss Turner,' Gently said. 'You've been very helpful. We appreciate it.'

He took his hat, rose. She looked up at him shyly.

'I'm glad,' she said. 'I told you about it. You're nice. I'm glad I told you.'

Then she began to cry.

'Give Johnny my love,' she said.

They went down the corridors, out into the thin October sunlight. Gently unlocked the Rover, they got in, he drove out of the park.

'He must have been waiting under the tree,' he said. 'I thought at first he was in that lane. But he couldn't have picked up the speed from there, so he must have been under the tree.'

'Yeah,' Setters said. 'Yeah.'

'He went after them without lights,' Gently said. 'Then at the last moment he switched them on, so he wouldn't be blind after he crashed them.'

Setters nodded at the windscreen. 'Oh Christ,' he said. 'I'm so sick of this.'

'We'll get back to Bixley,' Gently said.

He pressed a little harder on the gas.

At the desk they had a report for him from Brewer and Shepherd, the tails on Deeming. They'd picked him up in the High Street and followed him back to his rooms. He'd gone in and spent some time there, then he'd come out dressed for riding. He'd fetched his motor-cycle from a shed and parked it in the side lane leading to his rooms. Next he'd smiled at and saluted the policemen, and had gone off on foot to Everard's Restaurant. He was sitting there now eating his lunch. Brewer and Shepherd were also sitting there.

'Where's Everard's Restaurant?' Gently asked.

'Not far from where he lives,' Setters told him. 'It's in the street just round the corner. I eat there myself when I'm in a mood for eating.'

Gently hesitated. 'I'd like the patrols alerted,' he said. 'Give them Deeming's description and the description of his bike and tell them to keep watch out for him. If Brewer and Shepherd aren't right with him he's to be stopped and held for questioning.'

'Willco,' Setters said. 'But it's a good car and Brewer can drive.'

'So can Deeming,' Gently said.

'You should know,' said Setters.

They had a snack lunch sent into the office, sandwiches, fruit, and coffee. Gently ate his in silence, Setters made only odd remarks. There was something formidable about Gently when he didn't want to talk. He seemed a long way away, detached, out of reach. He finished his coffee.

'Can you spare half a dozen uniform men?' he asked.

'What to do?' Setters countered.

'To sit in here,' Gently said.

Setters shrugged. 'Window-dressing?'

'Yes,' Gently said. 'Window-dressing.'

'Huh,' Setters said. 'Well, I'll rustle you some up,'

The six men were found, instructed, and arranged in a semicircle in front of the desk. In the middle of the semicircle was placed a chair. On the desk was placed the flick-knife. Gently took the chair behind the desk. Setters sat to his right. Bixley was brought in, told to sit. The policemen drew their chairs up round him.

'So,' Gently said to him, 'you're back here again, Bixley.'

Bixley's mouth was tight, his cheeks flushed, his eyes frightened and unsteady. He threw a look at the policemen. They were all staring at him. He edged his chair towards the desk, saw the knife, went still.

Gently hit the desk hard.

Bixley jumped clear of the chair.

'You're nervous, Bixley,' Gently said. 'You've been eighteen hours without a smoke.'

Bixley shrank back on the chair. 'You can't do this, screw,' he croaked. 'I been charged, you can't touch me. It's the bleeding law, that is.'

'I didn't think the law mattered so much to you,' Gently said.

'Yuh,' Bixley said. 'You can't do it. None of you can't lay a finger on me.'

'Are you scared of something?' Gently asked.

'No,' Bixley said. 'I ain't scared.'

'You look scared,' Gently said.

'I ain't scared. Not of bleeding coppers.'

'I could understand it,' Gently said. 'There's a copper lying in the hospital. There's a girl lying there too. And there's one of your mates in the mortuary.'

'Yuh,' Bixley said. 'You don't scare me, screw.'

'You don't scare easily,' Gently said. 'I'd be scared if I were you.'

Bixley swallowed, touched the black bruise on the right side of his throat. Somebody behind him moved their chair. Bixley swung round, cringing. He met the hard stare of policemen.

'Yes,' Gently said. 'You're scared, Bixley.'

'You can't do it!' Bixley screamed. 'I want my rights. I want a lawyer!'

'Calm yourself,' Gently said.

'I been charged. I want a lawyer!'

'You haven't been charged,' Gently said. 'Not with murder. Not yet.'

'I ain't done no murder!' Bixley screamed. 'I ain't, you bleeding know I ain't.'

'We'll see about that,' Gently said. 'We'll see about a lot of things, won't we, Bixley?'

'You daren't touch me!' Bixley sobbed. 'You daren't do it. You bloody daren't.'

Setters turned his head over his shoulder and spat on the floor. 'Are you listening to me?' Gently asked.

'I never done it!' Bixley sobbed.

'Listen carefully,' Gently said. 'You're going to tell me all about that jazz session. And you're going to tell me the truth, because I'll know when you're lying, Bixley. And if you tell any more lies, fifty lawyers won't help you. So get it stuck in your head. Only the truth is any good.'

'I ain't done nothing,' Bixley sobbed. 'I ain't done nothing at all.'

'Sit up straight,' Gently said.

'I ain't, I ain't,' Bixley sobbed.

'Now, the truth,' Gently said.

'I ain't never killed nobody.'

'You'll have to prove it,' Gently said. 'Sit up straight and tell the truth.'

Bixley snivelled, propped himself up, began to stammer out his account. It didn't differ from earlier versions, he even left out the chocolates. Gently picked up the flick-knife, began stabbing at the paper with it. He let Bixley stumble on unquestioned till he'd faltered to a stop. Then he slammed the knife on the desk.

'Just run through it again,' he said.

Bixley gaped, didn't seem to hear him.

'Come on, come on,' Gently said.

'But I now told you—' Bixley began.

'Now tell me again,' Gently said.

One of the policemen shifted his feet. Bixley gulped, began to talk.

'That,' Gently said, 'didn't sound right either.'

'But it's the bleeding truth!' Bixley croaked. 'It is, I tell you.'

'You've left some things out.'

'No, I ain't!' Bixley said.

'Things,' Gently said, 'like how the counter-assistant told you who'd taken your box of chocolates.'

'It was Leach who told me!' Bixley screamed.

'My mistake,' Gently said. 'Now we'll run through it again, putting that bit in.'

They went through it again, putting that bit in. Bixley's lips were very dry, he slurred and tripped over his words. Setters was hammering a tattoo on the desk with his fingers. Bixley didn't like the sound. He didn't like Setters' eyes.

'So you knew,' Gently said, 'who'd gone off with your chocolates?'

'Yuh,' Bixley said. 'Yuh, yuh, I knew.'

'Yet you didn't go after him. You left a quarter of an hour later.'

'I thought I'd see him,' Bixley said. 'Yuh, I thought I'd see him around.'

'You thought you'd leave it like that – after just having paid forty quid for the chocolates?'

'Yuh,' Bixley said. 'Like that's what I did.'

'Though you knew he was going to shop you – that he was only waiting for the chance?'

'I didn't know nothing about that!' Bixley shouted. 'It's bleeding lies, all that is.'

'We've been talking to Betty Turner, Bixley.'

'I don't care. She's a bleeding liar.'

'Hallman too.'

'The bloody rat.'

'And there's a lot of others who knew about Lister.'

Bixley strained forward in the chair.

'All bloody right,' he croaked. 'All right. So Lister was going to put the squeal on me. Like I say, all bloody right!'

'And you didn't try to stop him,' Gently said.

'No, I didn't try to stop him!'

'You just let him go off with the box of reefers.'

'Yuh, yuh, I just let him go.'

'And Leach was lying if he said you telephoned.'

'I never telephoned!' Bixley screamed.

'Not to Tony's place?' Gently asked.

'I bleeding didn't. I bleeding didn't!'

'So there wouldn't be a record of such a call?'

Bixley gabbled out swear words.

'Deeming wants you hung,' Gently said. 'You know where you stand with Deeming, don't you?'

Bixley folded, began howling, stuck his palms in his

eyes. He rocked his shoulders from side to side, gasping out paroxysms like a kid.

'It ain't true!' he kept howling. 'It ain't true, you bloody swines!'

'It's true,' Gently said. 'You'd better take a look at where you stand, Bixley. We haven't got a thing on Deeming. We've got everything on you. You're scum. You're murderous scum. We'd sooner hang you than hang him. And you'll hang, Bixley, make no doubt of it, unless you can squirm out of it by ratting. So you'd better rat. It's your only chance. And you'd better pray that we believe you.'

'You're bloody lying!' Bixley howled. 'It ain't true, you dirty swine.'

'You'll hang,' Gently said. 'You've had your last chance, Bixley.'

He went on howling and screaming. Setters got up and walked about. The uniform men in their semicircle stared about them, looked uncomfortable. Only Gently never moved. He was leaning on his elbows on the desk. He watched the crumpled, hysterical, gang-boy with eyes completely empty of expression. His stillness was terrible. It was that which made Setters walk about.

Bixley half straightened, his eyes streaming. He clutched at the desk, held on to it. He crouched, his chin between his hands, his mouth open, gasping sobs.

'I didn't!' he sobbed, 'I didn't, I didn't, I didn't.'

'Deeming did,' Gently said. 'You phoned him. He did it.'

'Nobody did it,' Bixley sobbed. 'It was an accident, nobody did it.'

'Deeming did it,' Gently said. 'At your suggestion. You're in it with him.'

'No!' Bixley cried. 'I never suggested it. I didn't!'

'What did you suggest?' Gently asked.

'Not doing that,' Bixley sobbed.

'What else could you suggest?' Gently asked. 'Nothing else would have stopped Lister.'

'I didn't, I tell you,' Bixley sobbed. 'I never suggested anything at all.'

'What did you think Deeming would do?'

'I didn't think!' Bixley wailed.

'You must have thought,' Gently said.

Bixley went on howling.

The door was tapped. Setters strode over to it. The desk-sergeant stood there. He held a message slip in his hand, looked dubiously towards Gently.

'What is it?' Gently asked.

'It's a message from Brewer, sir,' the sergeant said. 'The bloke they were tailing has given them the slip. Brewer said to let you know directly.'

Gently sat silent for a moment, then he rose and took the slip. It was brief. Deeming had got clear in the café, he'd gone into the toilet and hadn't come out. After five minutes Brewer had gone after him and had found only an open toilet window. The window gave on a yard from which was access to Eastgate Street. Brewer had followed, found Deeming's motorcycle gone.

'Where are Brewer and Shepherd now?'

'Trying to pick up some trace of him, sir.'

'Tell them to come in, we need a car with R.T. And warn the patrols. They're to arrest Deeming on sight.'

'Yes, sir.'

The sergeant turned on his heel and went out. Gently pushed through the semicircle to Bixley, grabbed his collar and jerked him upright.

'You heard that, Bixley?' he said. 'Deeming's shaken off his tail. He's after Elton, Bixley – and Elton's your witness now.'

'I don't know nothing—!' Bixley squealed. The squeal was cut off by a violent shake.

'Listen!' Gently thundered at him. 'If Elton dies, you die. He's the only person who can save you. He can testify who killed Lister. And Deeming's after him, Bixley, Deeming wants you to hang. He's going to stop Elton talking the way he stopped Lister talking. Or is it that Elton's dead already?'

'He's alive!' Bixley screamed.

'Then where is he?' Gently roared. 'Where have you hidden him, Bixley?'

Bixley gurgled. Gently shook him and went on shaking him. Bixley let his muscles go limp and his head rolled about.

'Shuck's Graves!' he gasped at last. 'That's where, Shuck's Graves—!'

'Where?' Gently bawled in his ear.

'Shuck's Graves . . . Shuck's Graves!'

Gently dropped him, turned to Setters.

'Do you know where that is?' he asked him.

'Yeah,' Setters said, 'I know it. It's the place where Dicky took you on his bike.'

Gently stared. 'I'm a fool,' he said. 'Lock this one up, and let's get out there.'

CHAPTER THIRTEEN

BREWER DROVE. HE was a good driver, as Setters had said of him. He drove a safe nine on the Norwich road, had a steady touch, wasn't showy. When they turned off left into the side road he kept nibbling sixes in short stabs. He angled corners like a racing driver, straight in, straight out.

'I'm sorry, sir,' he'd said to Gently, who'd taken the seat beside him.

Gently had shrugged. 'You couldn't help it. And you didn't waste any time.'

Then, on purpose, he'd asked Brewer to drive, and Brewer was driving like a rally-winner. Shepherd was sitting intently behind them, Setters grimly in the other corner.

They came to the farm and its bumpy yard. Gently touched Brewer's arm. He slowed to a walking pace beside a run where a girl in breeches was cleaning a henhouse. Gently wound down his window.

'Has a motorcyclist passed this way, Miss?' he called.

She nodded, staring, scraper in hand. 'About ten minutes ago,' she called back.

'Thank you, miss.'

They bumbled away, struck the lane into the brecks. Over the dark swells, very far off, Gently caught sight of the two fir trees. All of them were eyeing the crests of those swells for a glimpse of a moving black speck. The light was silvery, flattening detail, dulling the contrast of the distance.

'You know this track?' Gently asked Brewer.

'Yes, sir, pretty well,' Brewer replied.

'Have you driven it to the main road at Five Mile Drove?'

'Yes, sir, a couple of times,' Brewer said.

Gently flicked the R.T. switch.

'X2 calling control,' he said. 'I want a car to intercept on the heath road running from Five Mile Drove to Shuck's Graves. Hold it a moment,' He returned to Brewer. 'Is there any other track to the Graves?' he asked.

'There's one from the north,' Brewer said. 'Comes in from Mundham and that way.'

'Could he use it?'

Brewer drove a moment. 'No,' he said. 'He couldn't get through. There's a mere out that way that floods in wet summers. We've had double the average. He couldn't get through.'

'Calling control,' Gently said. 'Put another car in Five Mile Drove. And cover Breck Farm Turn on the Norwich Road in case our man doubles back past us.'

'Received and understood,' control said. 'Willco. Out.'

The two fir trees got larger. There was no sign of

Deeming. Brewer hesitated once or twice where the track became uncertain. Sometimes it ran over a gravelly plateau from which departed several apparent alternatives, at other places heath grew over it, scars of pebbles offered themselves. Deeming had known the track better than did Brewer. He'd never hesitated once.

'We shan't be in time,' Setters bit out, goaded at last into breaking his silence. 'It won't take Deeming ten minutes. Elton's a kid, a lightweight.'

'Don't shoot the pianist,' Gently said.

'Yeah,' Setters said. 'Yeah, I know.'

He was holding the back of Gently's seat, trying to will the Wolseley to go faster.

They came at last to the top of the ridge where they could see the depression and the two hummocks. It looked deserted at first glance, and was quickly hidden as they ducked off the ridge. Then it came into sight again as the track approached the first hummock. There it was spread out in front of them, still, apparently, deserted.

'Where's the entrance?' Gently asked.

'Over in that far hillocky bit,' Setters said. 'It's been shut up since before the war. Since the archaeologists dug it.'

'Could anyone live in a place like that?'

'We'll soon see,' Setters snapped. 'For Chrissake, man,' he said to Brewer, 'keep driving – keep driving!'

Brewer turned off the track and bucked crazily towards the hummock. The surface of the depression was ribbed with gullies that sent the Wolseley pitching and porpoising. They'd covered a hundred yards of this and had another hundred to go when a couple of figures broke out of the hummock, seemed to rise out of the ground. One was Elton. He'd got blood on his head. The other was Deeming. He carried a spanner. Elton was screaming, running blindly, he didn't see the approaching Wolseley.

'Step on it, step on it!' Setters shrieked, standing up in the plunging car.

But Deeming had seen them, he'd dropped the spanner, was racing back towards the hummock. Elton saw them too, now, and seemed to be caught in two minds. He paused, wavered, began running towards the hummock with the fir trees.

'Go after Elton!' Gently shouted.

Brewer hung on the wheel, threw the Wolseley round. As he straightened it there came a roar from behind them and Deeming reappeared in the saddle of his motorcycle. Rising up on his rests, he floated past them over the broken ground, his machine bounding and jarring under him, himself steady, his knees springing. Elton heard him coming, turned, stood holding his hand out and screaming. Deeming went straight at him. Elton faltered sideways, was hit, went down.

He got up, ran a few paces, screaming piercingly all the while. He was holding his arm where he'd been hit. Deeming had turned and was going after him again.

'This way!' Gently roared. 'Make for us, Elton, make for the car!'

But Elton was confused, he was running chicken-like, this way and that.

Brewer stabbed down the accelerator in a violent attempt to intercept Deeming. The Wolseley rose up like a tank, crashed hard on its axles, bounded forward. Deeming avoided it easily. He rode at Elton standing high. Elton threw out his hands, dodged feebly, was hit on the shoulder, spun several yards.

Once more he got up, his face disfigured with pain and terror. Now it seemed he couldn't move, he stood swaying, wailing, crying. Deeming turned on him again.

'Stop the car!' Gently bawled.

But Setters was out before it stopped, went haring across to the paralysed Elton. He caught him up by the waist, snatched him aside from the oncoming bike. Brewer sent the Wolseley at Deeming. Deeming swerved, bore away. Setters dragged Elton towards the car, Shepherd jumped out, they lugged him in.

'He's going to kill me!' Elton was screaming. 'He's going to kill me, going to kill me!'

'He'll do some killing!' Setters panted. 'We'll string him up to that bloody fir tree.'

Deeming came round in a long curve, eased to a stop about thirty yards from the Wolseley. Gently opened his door, slid out. He began to walk towards Deeming.

'That's far enough, screw,' Deeming said when Gently was halfway towards him. He gave his throttle a touch, showed his teeth in a grin.

Gently stopped. They looked at each other. Deeming's slate eyes were glittering. The grin stayed on his face but the eyes weren't with it.

'Like you're asking for it,' Deeming said. 'I might

pick you off, screw. You get too far from that car and I could put you with Lister.'

'You'd better give yourself up,' Gently said.

Deeming gave an amused laugh. 'That wit,' he said. 'I always went for it big. Like why should I give myself up?'

'Because you're finished,' Gently said. 'We know the whole story, Deeming. You did for yourself when you came after Elton.'

'So I should give myself up?' Deeming said.

'It'll save you trouble,' Gently said. 'You're trapped. You can't get out. We've got cars covering all the exits.'

'Cars,' Deeming said. 'You funny screw.' He laughed again, stroked his throttle. 'You haven't cars enough,' he said, 'and they're kind of slow, kind of heavy. You can't get me with cars, screw. There isn't enough in all Squaresville. You can't touch me. I'm a free man. Better face it, screw. I'm free.'

'You'll get a fair trial,' Gently said.

'Surest thing,' Deeming said. 'It's nice to give a fair trial to a guy you're going to hang. Like then you can kind of rub it in, you can do the cat-and-mouse action. Squares love it, don't they, screw? They go for it big, a state kill.'

'You're a killer yourself,' Gently said.

'Yeah,' Deeming said. 'I'm a killer. But I don't kill in cold blood. I'm not as low as the squares, screw.'

'You knew the penalty,' Gently said.

'I know a lot about squares,' Deeming said. 'How come they don't like me killing, when they pay a murderer themselves?'

Gently shrugged. 'You'll have time to argue that out in your cell,' he said. 'But you can't get away, Deeming. We're going to pick you up somewhere.'

Deeming shook his head. 'Not you, screw. Not while I'm sitting on this bike. Take a look, screw. I'm a free man. Maybe you'll never see one again.'

'You aren't free,' Gently said.

Deeming chuckled. 'I'm free,' he said. 'As of now I've washed my hands of all squares and the taint of them. I'm on the borders now, screw. I'm reaching out for the big touch. I'm the only free man. You haven't got a weapon, screw.'

'I see you as a killer,' Gently said. 'A killer who's scared of the penalty.'

'Keep watching,' Deeming said. 'You've something left to learn yet.'

'You can't face it,' Gently said.

'Like I choose not to,' Deeming grinned. 'Free choice – you know? It's in my power to do either.'

There was a rush of feet behind Gently. Deeming hit his clutch, paddled away. Setters and Brewer, running like maniacs, tried to catch up with him and grab him. Deeming didn't put on speed. He let the two policemen stick close behind him. He rode a circle round the Wolseley, waited till first Setters, then Brewer, fell away. He continued riding back to Gently.

'See how it bounces?' he drawled. 'Like I've got the squares where I want them, tagging along in the rear.'

'So now what?' Gently said.

'Keep watching,' Deeming drawled. 'I wouldn't leave you in the lurch. Just keep your eyes stashed on Dicky.'

He curved off again, rode deliberately close to the advancing Setters, didn't swerve for an instant when Setters made a hopeful spring at him. Then he rode on to the track and pointed in the direction of the Chase. He kept going, very steady, at about fifteen miles an hour.

'Get into the car,' Gently said. 'There's nothing we can do except follow him.'

Setters flung himself in, breathing heavily and saying nothing. In the back of the car Shepherd was dabbing Elton's head with antiseptic. Elton had got his eyes closed. He was moaning and snivelling. He gave a wailing cry when the car started, made a fluttery, pushing motion with his hand. Gently pressed the R.T. switch.

'X2 calling control,' he said.

'Control receiving X2,' control said. 'Your patrols are on their stations.'

'We have Deeming under observation,' Gently said. 'He's proceeding along the track to Five Mile Drove. I want the two cars in that area to form a roadblock where the track goes through the Chase. Tell them to pick their spot carefully and to make sure it's completely blocked. Read it back. Over.'

Control read the message back.

'Further instruction,' Gently said. 'Tell them not to sit in the cars.'

They followed Deeming. He increased his speed when he found he had them behind him, established a distance of a quarter of a mile, settled down in the fours. Brewer made unobtrusive attempts to cut down on the distance, but they failed. Deeming was watching them closely in his mirror.

'What do we do when we come to the block, sir?' Brewer asked Gently.

Gently grunted. 'I'm wondering about that myself,' he said.

'We ram the louse,' Setters growled. 'Don't dare to let him come past you. If you fix him that's too bad. I'll cry all the way to the inquest.'

'Do you want him rammed, sir?' Brewer asked Gently.

'No,' Gently said. 'I want him in dock.'

Brewer frowned, held the speed steady, never let his eye stray from Deeming.

'He was going to kill me,' Elton moaned. 'He came there to kill me.'

Shepherd was flaking a bandage on him over a pad of moistened lint.

'They brought me food,' Elton said. 'I thought he'd come with my food. Then he hit my head. He was going to kill me.'

'We'll get him,' Setters said. 'Don't you worry, Elton.'

'I wouldn't have said nothing,' Elton said. 'I wouldn't never have said nothing. Then he hit my head. He pulled out a spanner and hit it. I fell down, he tripped over my feet. I got up the ladder and ran. I wouldn't have said nothing at all. But he was going to kill me.'

'Yeah,' Setters said. 'We know. Don't you worry about it, Elton.'

'He was nice to me,' Elton snivelled. 'Then he hit my head.'

Gently looked over his shoulder. 'Is that where the sticks are kept?' he asked.

'Yuh,' Elton blubbered. 'I never knew. That's where they kept them, down there.'

'Whose idea was it for you to hide there?'

'Sid Bixley's,' Elton said. 'He told me I was going to be arrested, I'd have to stop there till they fixed it.'

'Don't you worry,' Setters said. 'You're in the clear now, Elton.'

They began to see the Chase stretching sombrely across the skyline. Deeming hadn't changed his pace, was riding easily, relaxedly. A couple of times he'd looked back, given a derisive wave of his hand, but most of the time he just rode as though he were out for his pleasure.

Control called them up.

'Your block is in position, X2. About a mile from the main road, the track is closed off as instructed. Any further instructions?'

'Give me a supporting patrol,' Gently told them. 'Put it in Five Mile Drove, stationed at the junction with the track.'

'Willco,' control said. 'We'll try to send you another patrol.'

They came to the nursery, the fire-signs. A forest-ranger watched them go by. In the trees they lost sight of Deeming and Brewer promptly lifted his speed. Deeming let them come up closer. He wasn't trying to get away. He held them back at a hundred yards and Brewer settled down again. Setters was back holding the seat.

'Remember what I said,' he snapped at Brewer. 'You'll only be cheating the hangman, and we don't all like hangmen.'

'I'll try to stop him,' Brewer clipped.

'Better than that,' Setters said.

'Just stop him,' Gently said. 'If you can,' he added.

They cornered on a rise, went sweeping down a long straight. The block was just past the end of the straight. It was a very efficient block. The two cars were spread across the track, each bumper nested against a tree. The track was narrow and they more than filled it. Behind the cars stood their crews, watching.

Brewer stepped on the gas. They raced to close the gap on Deeming. He was trapped, he was slowing down. The men were running round to grab him. Brewer's lips were bundled tight, he was set to ram if necessary. But Deeming kept riding straight, didn't offer to break and double back.

Then his engine roared, he slanted right, dived headlong into the trees: slalomed crazily among the trunks of the tall, close-set pines. His rear wheel showered up dead pine needles, he was belting at full throttle. He jerked and twisted like a maddened animal, crashed through brushwood, reared back on the track. And then he was away, beyond the roadblock, shaking off a couple of pursuers. He cut his throttle, looked over his shoulder, made a mocking salute with five fingers.

The Wolseley skidded to a stop.

'Get these cars out of the way!' Gently shouted.

There was a rush for them and some awkward manœuvring before the block could be disentangled.

There was no room to pass: Gently switched cars, taking Brewer and Setters with him. Up the track Deeming sat on his bike, lit a cigarette, and grinningly waited.

They got away. So did Deeming: he performed a little victory roll. Brewer was pale and chewed his lip, made a hash of coming up through his gears.

'Oughtn't I to go after him?' he muttered to Gently.

Gently shook his head. 'It's a waste of time. Hold your speed in reserve. You'll never catch him in a straight run.'

Now only the support patrol waited ahead to try its luck with Deeming. If that failed, and he gained the road, they'd have to start planning afresh. Which way would he point if he reached the road? Away from Latchford, almost certainly. He would need to make for a town like Castlebridge, where he could lose himself in a maze of streets. Gently called control again.

'Deeming's got through the block,' he told them. 'We're observing him, but we can't catch him. I think he'll make towards Castlebridge.'

'Any instructions?' control came back.

'Yes,' Gently said. 'We'll have to try another block. There's a country house with park walls just this side of Oldmarket and I want the block at the Oldmarket end of the walls. From wall to wall, you understand? Don't leave the ditches uncovered. We'll have three or four cars behind him and should be able to stop him doubling.'

'Willco,' control said. 'We'll put Oldmarket on this one.'

From the back Setters rasped: 'You think that's going to get him?'

Gently grunted. 'No,' he said. 'But you have to go through the motions.'

The junction showed ahead, and there a fresh comedy was played. The support patrol saw Deeming, took off, drove steadily towards him. Brewer dutifully launched the Wolseley and the two cars rapidly converged on Deeming. Deeming feinted, sent the support car left, slid through right without raising his speed. Once more the track was blocked. For everyone except Deeming.

'All right!' Gently bellowed. 'Don't talk, just back out.'

The flustered driver of the support car lost his head, stalled his engine. He had to back a hundred yards to unbottle the other cars. It was ludicrous. Deeming might have been several miles on his way. Instead he sat jauntily watching from a position across the main road. If it was any comfort, he was pointed to Castlebridge. It didn't seem much comfort.

'Like you've got a good driver?' he shouted to Gently. 'You reckon he'll stay with me up here? You better climb on the pillion, screw, you better waltz with Matilda!'

'Give yourself up!' Gently shouted.

'Like I'm too valuable,' Deeming replied. 'But I'm sorry you can't be here behind me. Do your best, screw. Keep close.'

He pushed off, smoothed his throttle, began to sail away fast. Brewer didn't need telling. He was itching to let the Wolseley go. Gently sat deep in his seat, his eyes narrow, gone blank. Setters was leaning forward between them. He was breathing like a bloodhound. Still Deeming was going away from them.

'It's no good, sir,' Brewer clipped. 'He must have twenty miles an hour on us.'

'Keep at him,' Gently snapped.

The speedometer needle was pushing three figures.

There was traffic on the road. Deeming didn't care about traffic. He arrowed through it with little sways, kept near the centre of the road. Brewer had to notice the traffic. It pulled him down several times. Deeming got smaller and smaller ahead, a black atom of ferocious energy.

'Christ, to lose him like this!' Setters swore, dragging down on the seat backs. 'Playing with us all that time, then getting away like this. I could kick myself for it, I could bash my head on the wall.'

'Yes,' Gently muttered. 'We've lost him. He's beaten us.'

'He'll turn off,' Setters groaned. 'There's side-turns, plenty of them.'

'He won't turn off,' Gently said. 'He isn't going as far as a side-turn.'

Setters chewed on it for a moment. They were hitting the slight incline to the ridge. Brewer was hanging on to three figures though his engine laboured and shook.

'Come again with that?' Setters said.

'He's going to hit the tree,' Gently said. 'That's why he hasn't bothered to ditch us. We're going to be there to see it.'

'Hell,' Setters said. He stopped dragging, sank back on his seat. Brewer had heard what Gently said, his mouth thinned to a tight seam.

Setters came back, angling his face.

'You're serious about that?' he said.

Gently nodded. 'He's going to do it. He's had it in mind from the start.'

'But crying hell!' Setters said.

Gently said: 'I had the preview. He showed me just what he was going to do. He wanted to make sure I understood it.'

'Hell,' Setters said a third time.

'And we can't stop him,' Gently said. 'There he goes. A free man. He's beaten us all along the line.'

He was a long way off now, just a speck high up the road, weaving slightly and disappearing behind crawling, flashing cars. But the Gallows Tree was growing higher, was spreading its bare raven branches. The sky showed silver-white behind it, left it stark, hard, etched.

'He doesn't have to do it,' Setters said hoarsely. 'He's clear away. He could dodge us.'

Gently didn't say anything. Brewer kept murdering the engine.

'Maybe there's a case,' Setters said. 'He isn't normal. You can't call him normal.'

The tree stretched out massively, a dark, upward-rising torch.

It wasn't sensational. It was as though someone had thrown a bag of sweets at the tree. The sweets scattered, a few large ones, but most of them small. Only there'd been a firework in the bag and it shot up a yellowish pillar of flame, and off the top of the pillar lifted black smoke, going up straight in the still air.

He'd been half a minute ahead of them, enough to

collect a jam of traffic. Brewer drove in hooting frenziedly, squealed the Wolseley to a stop. They jumped out, ran across. A white-faced man was using an extinguisher. Another was lugging at a riding-boot. It came away. He collapsed in a faint. The body was tangled with the frame of the bike, it was being burned. The tree was burning.

'Get away, all of you!' Gently ordered. 'You can't do any good here. Leave the rest of this to us – on your way, on your way!'

'He was laughing,' said the man with the extinguisher. 'That's my car . . . I saw him do it. I could see his teeth. He was laughing. You won't believe me. But he was laughing.'

'Drive on a bit,' Gently said. 'We'll talk to you later, drive on a bit.'

'I saw him laughing,' the man said. 'I know that nobody's going to believe me.'

The tree was catching all the way up, it was useless attacking it with extinguishers. Brewer was back with the R.T. summoning an ambulance and a fire engine. There was no dispersing the gapers. Even the smell wasn't shifting them. The smoke had puffed up to a great height, it must have been visible for many miles.

'What a way to do it,' Setters was babbling. 'Oh, my God, what a way to do it.'

The flames were snarling and becoming redder, smuts dropped out of the noisome smoke.

CHAPTER FOURTEEN

IT WASN'T THEIR job to pick up the pieces. They left when the firemen had doused the flames. The tree was still standing, though badly charred; it was obviously a danger and would have to come down. But just now it continued to stand there, spectre-like, laced with foam. From the end of the Drove it had a piebald look as though it were stricken with a leprous disease.

They ate at H.Q., another scrappy sandwich meal. Setters got some wheels turning and fixed the inquest for the morrow. Elton had been taken to the hospital – one more casualty; but he had only bruises and a scalp contusion and he wasn't detained. He came back to make a short statement. The statement was confirmatory. He told them how Deeming had searched Lister's wrecked bike for the box of reefers. Sergeant Ralphs had revisited Shuck's Graves, had removed from them eight thousand reefers. He brought back the spanner Deeming had dropped. It had blood and some hairs adhering to it.

'So nobody gets hung,' Setters said, weighing the

spanner in his hand. 'Bixley can wriggle out of this one, less a few years in Norwich clink.'

'They're experimenting at Norwich,' Gently said. 'They're trying to rehabilitate their prisoners.'

'Fine,' Setters said, 'fine. They've got some bonza material coming.'

He studied the spanner for some moments, solemnly, before he locked it away in his desk; lit his umpteenth cigarette and let it hang on his lip.

'I feel I've been through it,' he said. 'You ever get that feeling?'

Gently nodded. 'Violence isn't very funny,' he said.

'Yeah,' Setters said. 'That's it. Violence isn't very funny. It reads well, doesn't act. You can't play it for a laugh. And what makes you so sick is you can't get rid of it. It's there, we've all got it. That's what makes you so sick.'

'Don't look at me,' Gently said. 'I don't have any answer. You can't hang it, you can't flog it, and you can't lock it up.'

'You just live with it,' Setters said. 'It goes on, and you live with it. You can't preach it away neither. We don't know a damn thing.'

'Perhaps we're misusing it,' Gently suggested. 'Perhaps there's a channel for it somewhere. It's a bit of nature we've inherited and don't understand.'

'I don't understand it,' Setters said. 'I thought I did up till now. But I get pretty close to Bixley. I could bust out too.' He stuck his hands in his pockets.

'Come on,' he said. 'Let's shut the door.'

⋆ ⋆ ⋆

MOTORCYCLIST DIES ESCAPING
SUSPECTED OF LISTER MURDER
TIE–UP WITH BIG DOPE SEIZURES

After an exciting chase after an exciting chase after an exciting chase after an exciting chase after an exciting chase

★ ★ ★

So this big-shot screw came down from the Smoke, started making with the action like he could figure the whole deal. There were some sticks going about, he latched hard on them, man. Threw a curve they were the reason for Johnny Lister taking off. First he hung up Sid Bixley, wild keen he was on Sid. But like Sid was too good for him, he knew the jazz to hand screws. Then this crazy big-shot goes for Dicky, wild, way-out Dicky Deeming, the mostest guy who ever cooled it on a ton plus action. Man, did Dicky give them a ride. Like they'll never forget about Dicky. One of the jees makes with a ballad about Wild Dicky Deeming.

Came the day when this big-shot reckons he'll hang Dicky up. Gets him a car with a cool wheel-man and a couple more screws for ballast. Dicky's right there in the eatery when they decide on the hang-up, but like they never get a finger on him, he walks clear past a pair of them. So they make with the car, man, they cool it big after Dicky. They chase him out to Shuck's Graves, way over on the heath. And Dicky's sat there waiting for them. He laughs his lid off at these screws. He rides around playing tag with them, sits ribbing them when they're puffed.

Then away rides Dicky with the screws chasing after him. He's too crazy, they can't fetch him, they buzz a lot more

screws. So there's like six or seven of these cars piling up to stop Dicky, and all the screws stood around, they're going to hang him up for sure. And up Dicky rides, don't turn a hair at these screws. Like they tumble over their feet to put a grab on Dicky. So Dicky laughs crazy wild, goes dodging around in the trees, and the next thing the screws know he's way up on the other side of them.

Then the screws are real mad, they'll do next to anything to hang up Dicky. They buzz the other screws for miles, it's stiff with screws charging about. And Dicky, he's leading a whole bunch of them, keeps playing it down to hold them together. He's getting the wildest kicks, is Dicky. He's picking up screws all along. So then he has them out on the road, half the screws in the country. Tells them he's going for the touch, like they can tag along if they want to. And then he twists it man, he goes man, he leaves the screws dragging backwards. He comes to the tree, he keeps going. He touches the real all the way.

You want to know about the curves the screws threw when Dicky touched? Man, they've got a curve for everything, like they daren't not have. They hung up a jee called Elton, pitched him around something rotten, got him sounding off some jazz about Dicky busting into Lister. Yuh, that's the curve they threw, like somebody ought to believe them. And the army squares cut the tree down. Let on it was dangerous, or some jazz.

But I'll tell you something, man, and the squares know about it too. There's a guy called Salmon used to live here and he was riding that road one night. Come back late from a dance, he was, and cooling it wild down the road. And like there was somebody riding beside him. Somebody who didn't make a sound. And he was grinning at him, waving him on. And Salmon could see the tree right plain. And he got a smell in his nose like burning mutton and he threw up twice before he could stop.

Yuh, it's spooky round this scene, I like it daylight when I'm riding. There's Johnny and Dicky died on the road, and the road gets quiet. I like it daylight.

Brundall, 1960